Six Ways of Dying

In his wildest dreams, Angelo never imagined he would forge such an unusual partnership with an old man, two tough brothers, their hired gunmen . . . and a treasure map. Though it had started well, in less time than it takes to cock a Colt the whole deal was going bad.

Determined to get even, Angelo sets out to track down the men who double-crossed him. Only this time, he is saddled with an arrogant cavalry officer, some raw recruits and a beautiful girl – with whom he has fallen helplessly in love.

Upon meeting Ulzana, the Apache renegade, they find themselves outnumbered and exhausted. But Angelo doesn't give a damn about the odds. If he has to go down, he'll go down fighting.

Six Ways of Dying

Cody Wells

ROBERT HALE · LONDON

First published in Great Britain 2011

ISBN 978-0-7090-9328-2

Robert Hale Limited
Clerkenwell House
Clerkenwell Green
London EC1R 0HT

www.halebooks.com

Typeset by
Derek Doyle & Associates, Shaw Heath
Printed and bound in Great Britain by
CPI Antony Rowe, Chippenham and Eastbourne

For Sherry Negrete
She's my inspiration

CHAPTER ONE

For Angelo it had been a long, slow ride from the small town of Gatlin to the West Texas military outpost of Fort Conchos, but he was in no great hurry. As he made camp, a gentle breeze blew dust across the prairie. It was almost sundown and the sky cast a serene crimson glow across the land.

He took a mouthful of coffee. He'd been watching the rider heading towards him for the past half-hour. As the newcomer drew closer Angelo could see that he was astride a large mule that seemed to be giving him trouble. It came to an abrupt halt, and shook its head. The rider threw his arms in the air and appeared to be cursing the animal.

'Can you believe that?' muttered Angelo, rubbing the nape of the dog lying by his side. 'Folk would say *our* relationship was strange.'

The dog was an odd-looking thing; mostly Canaan but with a little something else thrown in. He had wolflike features, but his cream-white coat was much smoother, his snout shorter. Low-set ears and a bushy tail completed the picture.

Angelo gave the beans cooking over the small fire a vigorous stir. After cussing the animal some more, the newcomer finally slid from the saddle and tried desperately to get the mule to move.

'Yer selfish and stubborn. If'n I didn't need ye so bad, I'd make jerky out of yer hide.'

The animal kicked its hind legs in the air, then took off across the prairie. The man took off his hat, threw it on the ground and stamped on it.

'Come back here, ye sumbitch . . . Damn mule!'

When the man was about twenty yards from Angelo's camp he called, 'Mind if I join ye, young 'un?'

He was in his mid-sixties and about five and a half feet tall. His hair was as white as snow, and matched his beard. He wore an old gray cavalry slouch hat, the brim pinned up at the front with a brass crossed-saber insignia. The red bib-shirt was worn with the top and two side buttons undone, and his black wool pants were held up by white canvas suspenders.

'Come on in, old-timer,' Angelo called back. 'Take some warmth from the fire.'

The old man smiled, revealing toothless gums. 'Thanks son. I just needs to rest me a while, then I'll be on my way.'

As he came in he studied his host more closely. The man by the fire was a dark-skinned half-blood who'd seen maybe thirty-five summers. He stood a lean six feet two, with high cheekbones, a strong jaw and raven-black hair that tumbled to his shoulders. He wore a wine-colored cotton shirt and buff canvas pants that were faded with age, and his low-crowned Stetson was pulled down slightly at the front to shadow his blue, hawk-sharp eyes. He packed a short-barreled but fancily engraved Colt Peacemaker .45 in a brown Mexican single-looped holster on his right hip.

'Looks like that mule of yours just won the argument,' Angelo noted.

'He's one ornery son-of-a-gun. I swear, the night he wus born he wus blessed by the devil himself. Yeah . . . he's kinda off his mental reservation.'

The old man was just about to sit next to the dog when it stood up and growled. Angelo said, 'This here's Mr Jinx. I wouldn't get too close if I were you. He don't take kindly to strangers.'

The old man took a red bandanna from his pants' pocket and used it to pick up the hot coffee pot from the fire. 'Mind if I pour myself a cup?'

'Go ahead,' Angelo said as he pulled another cup

from his sack of supplies and handed it to the old man.

'You gotta name, son?'

'Angelo. You?'

'Jebediah Tumbleweed O'Malley. Most folks jus' call me Tumbleweed.'

'Tumbleweed! What kind of a name is that?'

The old man raised his eyebrows. 'When I wus born, my pa said a baby around the farm wus as much use as tumbleweed. So the name sorta stuck. Guess it must have bin his Irish sense of humor.'

'What you gonna do about that mule of yours?' Angelo asked.

'Ah, he'll turn up in the mornin'. He always does. My place is about eight miles down the trail there. It's not much, but I call it home.'

Angelo threw the old man a spare blanket. 'Well, why don't you get your head down here for tonight? Then we can double up on my horse in the mornin' and I'll take you home.'

'Well that's mighty kind of ye, son. Happen I'll take ye up on that.'

O'Malley's place, when they reached it the following morning, wasn't much to speak of, just a small shack set well back from the main trail, with a corral and a lean-to at the far end. Twenty feet from the shack stood an outhouse with a sign nailed to the door that read TRESPASSERS WILL BE SHOT! A vegetable patch lay to the right of the corral, where the mule was making a meal out of whatever had been planted.

Tumbleweed slid from Angelo's horse and ran towards the beast, waving his hands in the air. 'Ye sumbitch, git the hell outta thur, ye dumb mule!'

The spooked animal ran off into the corral with Tumbleweed close behind. The mule walked up to the lean-to and took a long drink from the water trough. The old man secured the gate.

'I swear, one of these doggone days, I'm gonna blow what little brains he's got all over this darn prairie.'

Angelo climbed down from the saddle and tied his horse to the hitching rail in front of the shack. The front door was ajar. The old man sauntered in and gave out a loud yell.

Joining him in the doorway, Angelo peered over the old-timer's shoulder and saw that the whole room was in disarray. The few bits of furniture had been damaged, the shelves cleared of the pots, pans and cooking supplies, which were now scattered all over the floor. Tumbleweed's personal belongings and clothes were covered in cooking oil and flour.

'Looks like that mule of yours really has it in for you,' Angelo commented wryly.

'Mule, my ass . . . I've bin robbed!' He scurried

up to the stove. It had been shifted to reveal a small hole in the floor, just big enough to fit a small box. 'Sumbitch!'

'What's up, old man?'

'Some varmint's stole my darn map! That's wut's up!'

'Map?'

'Wus a treasure map,' the old man said, adding quickly, 'An' don't gimme that look. My map wus the real thing. I just knows it wus.'

Just then Mr Jinx tugged at Angelo's shirt-cuff and barked to get his attention. Turning, he saw that six mounted men were riding in at a slow, steady pace. Six dangerous-looking men.

'We've got company, old man.'

Tumbleweed came to join him. 'Darn it, if it ain't Tom and Quincy Randall.'

'Friends of yours?'

'Pains in the ass, more like.'

'You got any guns around this place?'

'Got myself a Colt coach gun lyin' around somewhurs, if I kin find it amongst this here mess.'

'Fetch it.'

As the old man went in search of his gun Angelo went outside and slid his Winchester from its scabbard, all the while keeping a steady gaze on the approaching men, with Mr Jinx sitting by his side. As the riders brought their horses to a halt in front of the shack Tumbleweed came running through the doorway.

'Got it! Wut now?'

Angelo gave the strangers a cold stare. 'See that burly fella in the white shirt?'

'Yeah, I see him. That thur's Quincy.'

'Well, old man, if Quincy so much as blinks an eyelid, blast him out of his saddle.'

'That's no way to greet friends!' Quincy bellowed. He was a robust specimen in his early forties, with a round face and small piggy eyes. His auburn hair was short and he wore a bushy mustache and long sideburns. He wasn't a tall man, five and a half feet, but what he lacked in height, he made up for in muscle. His attire was nothing out of the ordinary: blue denim pants, white cotton shirt and a brown suede vest. He wore a gunbelt with the holster tied down on his left thigh.

'You're no friend of mine,' Angelo said. 'So state your business or move on out.'

'No need to take that attitude, mister. We've known Tumbleweed since we were knee-high to a grasshopper. We're all friends here. Ain't that right, old-timer?'

'Go to hell!' Tumbleweed snarled.

It was true, however, that Tumbleweed had known the brothers for years. Quincy and Tom, who was his junior by barely ten months, made a dubious living by hanging around the cattle auctions in town and preying on unsuspecting businessmen who didn't know one end of a cow from the other. They made the deals and took a fat percentage from the businessmen for their questionable 'guidance'.

'Get to it,' said Angelo.

Quincy leaned forward. 'Well, it's like this. We were passing here late yesterday, when we noticed that you had visitors. Well, me and the boys here chased 'em off, but not before they could make a mess an' all. When we checked around I came across what looked like a map lying on the floor.'

Tumbleweed pulled back both hammers on the shotgun. 'Yer a no-good thievin' sumbitch, Quincy, an' a liar to boot! I oughta blow yer brains out.'

'Take it easy, old man. Just listen to what I've got to say,' Quincy said. 'Mind if we climb down awhile?'

'Yup.'

'OK, have it your way. Now, we both know there's gold buried somewhere around these parts. You know the place, and I know how many paces and in which direction. Put 'em both together . . . and what do we have? A partnership.'

Angelo glanced at Tumbleweed and muttered, 'Will someone please tell me what the Sam Hill's going on here?'

'Nuthin', that's wut,' said the old man. He stamped over to Quincy. 'Supposin' I just sit tight and say nuthin'?' he countered. 'Ye'll never git yer hands on it. How's 'bout that?'

'Then neither will you, old man,' Quincy snarled.

'Well, I guess there's nothin' left to talk about,' said Angelo.

Quincy threw him a withering stare. Then: 'I'll be back, you old coot, you can count on it.' Quincy turned his horse and spurred it into a gallop. The others followed suit.

The two men watched until the riders were just specks in the distance. Then Angelo placed his hand on the old man's shoulder. 'You gonna be all right, old-timer?'

'Ah, don't ye worry 'bout me, son. Them thur brothers are full of cow dung. They ain't gonna do nuthin'. I'll be fine.'

Angelo slid the rifle into the boot and climbed into the saddle. He leaned down and extended his hand. 'Well, I guess I'll be on my way. You take care of yourself, and don't let that mule get the better of you.'

Tumbleweed shook Angelo by the hand. 'If yer ever in the area, drop in and we'll share a jug of Honest John.'

Angelo laughed. 'Sure, old man, we'll do that. So long!'

CHAPTER TWO

Around midday Angelo decided to spell himself and his horse along the banks of the Concho River. There was an oak tree near to the water's edge and he slid from the saddle and allowed his horse to drink. After tending to its needs, he took shelter under the shade of the tree with Mr Jinx lying beside him, panting heavily to cool off, but he couldn't shake the feeling that had been nagging at him ever since he and Tumbleweed had parted their ways.

'You know, boy, I can't get that old man out of my head. I've the darndest feelin' that he's headin' for a heap of trouble.' The dog gave a short woof. 'You think so too, huh?'

The dog stood up and wagged his tail.

'OK, OK. We'll go back and see what he's up to. I just hope I don't live to regret it!'

He felt a shiver run down his spine as he rode up to Tumbleweed's shack. There were six horses tethered out front, and raised voices coming from inside. He climbed from the saddle and took out his rifle. Holding the Winchester close to his chest, he put his back to the wall next to the front window and listened carefully to what was being said inside.

Quincy's voice was urgent. 'It don't make sense, all that gold just sittin' there and no one makin' a move to claim it. Why're you being so stubborn, you old fool? Just tell us where the location is so we can use the map.'

'Do ye think I wus born yesterday? If'n I tell ye whure it is, wut use would I be to ye after that?' Tumbleweed countered.

'You think we'd do you harm, old man?' Quincy chuckled. 'You have us all wrong! We want to share the gold with you. Like I said earlier . . . partners.'

'Yeah, partners until my back's turned, thun I'd be pushin' up daisies.'

Quincy grabbed the old man by the front of his shirt. 'Listen, you old coot, you'd better start talkin' or I'm gonna lose my temper!'

Angelo had heard enough and he kicked open the door. Startled, Quincy's brother Tom went for his gun but Angelo brought the Winchester's butt up and around, crushing his nose like it was a peach. As Tom squealed and dropped his gun,

Angelo leveled the rifle on Quincy. Beside him, Mr Jinx bared his teeth.

'Never thought I'd see ye again, son,' Tumbleweed said with obvious relief, scurrying to Angelo's side.

Quincy meanwhile went to his brother's aid. 'You sonofabitch, just look what you've done! There was no need for that!'

Angelo ignored him. He knew the old man wouldn't get any peace until this business was settled once and for all. 'OK, Tumbleweed, let's hear all about this gold. Might be best all round if we do.'

Tumbleweed looked towards Quincy, then scratched his head. 'I'll tell ye, but I'll be darned if I tell ye the exact location whur the gold is hidden. How'll that be?'

'That'll be just fine, old man.'

Tumbleweed went over to the fireplace and rummaged around his bits and pieces and picked up a clay pipe. 'It were two years after the war, and I wus a scout at Fort Chadbourne. There wus a young half-breed by the name of Charlie Two-Shoes. I kinda liked the young 'un. He would often talk to me 'bout the days when he used to go huntin' with his pa, and helped his ma with the daily chores. But Charlie used to have these nightmares 'bout the time whun his life wus turned upside down. See, one day a bunch of drunken cowpokes stopped by their cabin. They called his ma a dirty Comanche whore an' then raped and butchered her, and made the young 'un watch as they tortured his pa and killed him.'

Tumbleweed drew in smoke.

'Anyways, me and the young 'breed got on well together. The Comanche scouts saw him as a white man and didn't trust him. The soldiers saw him as a son of a Comanche whore and wouldn't talk to him, less'n it wus fer scoutin' information. Me, though, I always saw him as a friend.

'Fort Chadbourne wus comin' to an end, and they wanted to build a new fort along the Concho River. They sent a team of surveyors out to the proposed site, along with a detail of soldiers. They also sent out a couple of scouts. Charlie wus one of 'em.

'When they got to the site and the surveyors began their work, young Charlie was ordered to clean up the area where a couple of old wagons had been abandoned years before. The wheels were broken and the wood was rotten, so he decided to smash the wood up and burn it. But whun he comes to the second wagon, he found a secret compartment in the floor. They was four ammunition boxes with CSA markin's. At fust Charlie thought nuthin' of it, just dragged the boxes from the wagon and opened one of 'em. There, starin' him in the face was twenty small unmarked gold bars!'

'So all four boxes had twenty bars of gold in 'em?' Quincy asked excitedly.

'Yep.'

'What did he do next?' Angelo asked.

'Well, seein' as it was Confederate gold, it would be classed as treasure . . . finders' keepers. Charlie'd seen wut gold could do to a man, and so's not to cause a gold fever amongst the troops, he buried it. No-one took any notice as to wut he was doin'. The soldiers took shelter in their tents and played cards or slept, while the surveyors did their work.'

'How come you ended up with the map?' Angelo asked. 'And how do you know that Charlie didn't make the whole thing up?'

Tumbleweed wandered over to the pantry and dragged out a sack of flour. He dug deep into the contents and pulled out a heavy parcel wrapped in brown paper. Looking Quincy right in the eye he said, 'Somethin' ye fellas missed whun ye was here the first time.' He undid the package to reveal two small gold bars. '*Now* do ye believe me?'

Angelo took one of the bars and checked it over. There was no doubt about it, they were the genuine article, and must have been worth a small fortune.

Tom Randall forgot all about his busted nose and took a close look at the gold. 'We could never spend all that gold in a lifetime, even if we did split it six ways!'

'I think yer all forgettin' somethin',' growled Tumbleweed. 'That thur buried gold is techne – technal – technic . . . it's darn well mine. And it stays thur unless we can make a fair deal.'

'What do you call fair?' asked Quincy.

'We'll split it fifty-fifty. I'll share mine with my friend here,' the old man said. 'Ye can split yer share whichever way ye please.'

'Why can't we just split it eight ways?'

'I'm not gonna argue 'bout it, Randall. Take it or leave it.'

'All right, you sonofabitch, have it your way . . . fifty-fifty. Now let's get some shovels and go dig it up.'

Tumbleweed scratched his beard. 'It ain't gonna' be that easy, fellas.' He walked over to Quincy and held out his hand. 'Give me the map an' I'll show ye wut the problem is.'

Quincy hesitated. 'You better not be trying to double-cross me, old man.'

'I'm not.'

Reluctantly he handed the map over. Tumbleweed unfolded it and pointed to the symbols that Charlie had drawn. There were a tree, four drawings of the sun and lots of crosses.

'See this here tree?' he said. 'Wull, the cross-marks go left four paces, right ten paces, right three paces and left five paces and so on! Charlie made it so ye would need the map, as no one would ever remember all the steps an' directions.'

Tom could hardly contain himself. 'All right,' he said nasally. 'So where's the tree?'

'Thur lies the problem. It's slap bang in the middle of Fort Concho!'

Quincy frowned. 'You mean to say the gold is in the *fort*? Are you serious?'

'Darn right I'm serious. Three weeks after Charlie Two-Shoes buried it, they began to build the new fort in the exact same location as the gold. Lucky for us they left the tree intact.'

Angelo laughed. 'Well, I guess that's the end of that!'

Quincy rubbed his chin vigorously. 'Let's not be too hasty. There has to be a way around this.'

'That gold's buried on Federal land. If we get caught with it, we're each lookin' at a minimum of twenty years' hard labor,' Angelo said grimly.

'Yeah – *if* we get caught! I say let's go for it. If your friend here don't want in, Tumbleweed, that's his loss.'

'I'll talk him round,' said Tumbleweed.

He led Angelo out into the sunshine and over toward the corral, where they wouldn't be overheard. Before he could speak, however, Angelo said, 'I'm no saint, Tumbleweed, but everythin' I've done up till now has been honest. I don't intend crossin' that line, old-timer.'

'Ye don't have to, ye darn fool!'

'What do you mean?'

'Ever heard of a finder's fee? Reward fer finding treasure?'

Understanding finally dawned and Angelo gave a low, admiring whistle. 'Well, you sneaky old goat! You intend get the gold and turn it in for a reward?'

' 'Course that's wut I mean. But don't ye go tellin' them bastards inside. Let that be a surprise fer 'em.'

'My lips,' said Angelo, 'are sealed.'

CHAPTER THREE

Before they could do anything else they had to get inside the fort without arousing suspicion. Stagecoaches and settlers often stopped there before traveling further south to Santa Angela. But Angelo and his companions needed a reason to stick around for a while, and to do some digging.

'I think I've got it,' Angelo said after a few minutes. 'Supposin' one of us was to pretend to be some kind of government official, say he'd been sent to check for sinkholes or somethin'?'

Tumbleweed's eyes lit up. 'Ye might just have somethin' thur, big 'un. But I reckon we can do better'n that sinkhole crap. I know fer a fact the colonel's bin askin' fer a hospital an' school fer the kids. So far his requests have always been denied.'

'So our government man'll be an architect, then, there to draw up plans for exactly what the colonel wants,' Quincy decided.

'It'll sure get him on our side,' Tom agreed. 'If he thinks it'll get him what he wants, he'll bend over backwards to accommodate us.'

'Who plays the official?' asked Angelo, not caring much for the idea of building the soldier's hopes up only to dash them again.

'You do,' said Quincy. Catching Angelo's look he explained, 'You're the only one who isn't known in these parts.'

'Well, fer once I'll have to agree with Quincy here,' muttered Tumbleweed. 'Yer the only one of us that looks halfway honest. An' ye could say that ye hired us as yer laborers.'

Angelo's lips thinned down. But if Quincy was right, he *was* their best bet. After giving the matter some thought he said, 'All right, I'll give it a whirl. But I can't ride in like this. If I'm gonna play the part, then I've got to *look* the part.'

'Ye'll need a suit,' said Tumbleweed.

'And a haircut,' gloated Tom.

Angelo threw him a withering glance. But again, he knew it made sense. Much as he preferred to wear his hair long, it was going to have to come off, leastways for a while.

'We'll wait for you here,' said Quincy. 'Then we'll all ride to the fort together.'

'*You* can wait,' said Angelo. 'But I'll take Tom

along with me.'

'Why?'

'Because I don't trust you, Quincy. I don't trust any of you. I keep you brothers apart, I keep you from cookin' up any schemes against me and the old man. Besides, we'll need a wagon and team: tools, too. Tom can buy everythin' while I'm gettin' scalped.'

Tumbleweed put the gold back into the flour sack. 'I'll tag along wuth ye, if that's OK?'

'You gonna trust us to sit here with that gold lyin' around?' Quincy said wryly.

Tumbleweed laughed. 'I know ye only too well. Why steal two bars of gold whun thur's another seventy-eight waitin' to be dug up?'

As they headed for town, Angelo again found himself wondering just what he was letting himself in for. He'd never been a greedy man. Like 'most everyone else, he'd only ever craved a dollar more than he could spend. And here was a chance to make good money, legally. But still something sat uneasily with him. He didn't care much for the subterfuge involved, of promising this here colonel a school and hospital that would never materialize.

Like just about every army town, Santa Angela had more than its share of brothels, saloons and gambling houses. The town bustled with activity as the three men rode down Main Street. Boisterous voices and loud music poured from the saloons. Angelo reined his gelding and brought it to a halt in front of the Golden Horseshoe.

'This'll do fine,' he announced as he slipped from the saddle and tied his horse to the hitching rail.

'We're goin' in here?' Tom asked.

'This is where we're leavin' our mounts,' corrected Angelo. 'You got chores that don't involve whiskey, Tom. Just go buy us a halfway decent rig an' team, an' tools for diggin'. An' Tumbleweed?'

'Yup?'

'Make sure he don't pay any more than he has to.'

'Wull, ye just take ye time, son. We'll be fine,' Tumbleweed said as he checked to see how much cash he had on him.

'An' remember,' Angelo added sternly, 'we don't want to attract any unnecessary attention. Got that?' He fixed them with a hard look, then added, 'Take Mr Jinx with you.'

Tom watched Angelo cross the road and head for the bank. Then he turned and headed for the saloon. Tumbleweed grabbed him by the arm and said, 'Hey, thur! Ye heard wut Angelo said!'

'The day I take orders from that sonofabitch is the day you can bury me in the stone-cold ground,' Tom replied, and shoved through the batwings.

Tumbleweed sighed, then glanced down at the dog and followed him inside.

The place reeked of stale tobacco and kerosene. The barroom was smaller than most, just enough room to fit six sets of tables and chairs, all of which were occupied. Five soldiers stood around a piano player who was whipping out an awkward version of 'Oh Susannah'. They were all so well-oiled that it was a struggle for them to sing in tune.

There was a small bar in the far corner of the room next to the stairwell. A scrawny, bald-headed man stood behind it, polishing glasses with a dirty towel. He cracked a professional smile as they bellied up. 'Name your disturbance, fellers.'

'Gimme a bottle of whiskey,' said Tom. 'The good stuff.'

'Tell ye what,' said the barkeep. 'I got a new batch in yesterday. Real Scotch whiskey, brewed in Kentucky.'

'I don't care what it is, as long as it don't steal my sight,' Tom said.

Tumbleweed prodded Tom on the arm. 'The big fella said to keep a low profile.'

'So, what's your point?'

'Wull, it's a known fact that ye and yer brother can't hold yer liquor to save yer lives.'

'Ah, quit your gripin', old man.'

The barman put the bottle of whiskey on the

counter, took payment and went back to rearranging the smears on his dirty glasses.

At the bank, meanwhile, Angelo withdrew enough money to shop with. He had saved a sizeable amount over the last three years, almost $10,000, and he'd earned every penny of it. At one of the small outfitters he managed to find himself a decent suit which was an almost perfect fit. He also treated himself to a new shirt and tie, along with a derby hat that went perfectly with the newly acquired garments. He had his old clothes wrapped in brown paper and took them with him when he left.

All that remained was the ticklish matter of his haircut. For a man of his free-and-easy sensibilities, that was going to hurt. He found a tonsorial parlor and took his place in the barber's chair. The barber, a fat man with black curly hair around an otherwise hairless crown, asked him what he wanted. Angelo shrugged uncomfortably. 'I don't know. What's all the rage these days?'

'I should say the pompadour,' came the reply. 'Swept back from the forehead, worn quite tall, perhaps with muttonchops?'

Angelo grimaced. 'Just cut it short, oil it and give me a centre part.'

Afterwards, as he made his way to the Golden Horseshoe, he stopped outside a baker's shop and used the window as a mirror to admire his new look. It would take some getting used to, but he reckoned he'd manage it in time. He put the parcel down on the sidewalk and adjusted his hat, then stood back, tilting his head from left to right.

'My, my. Did you know that vanity is one of the cardinal sins?'

He turned quickly to see a young lady smiling at him as she prepared to mount her horse. She was in her mid-twenties, and in bare feet would stand about five and a half feet tall. Her large brown eyes looked the tall man up and down, which made him feel a little uneasy. She wore a white cotton blouse, and tight-fitting pants which left little to the imagination. Her auburn hair, cascading down over her left shoulder, was pushed forward by the fullness of her breast under her tight-fitting blouse.

'Ma'am?' Angelo managed in a strangled voice.

The young lady gave no reply, just climbed into the saddle and spurred the sorrel into a lope.

As he bent to pick up his package he heard a sudden flurry of cries and curses coming from the Golden Horseshoe. A burly soldier came running through the swing doors, holding the shredded crotch of his pants and yelling for a doctor. Another soldier crashed through the front window and landed on the sidewalk, his face covered in glass-cuts. Just as Angelo came level with the doorway, the batwings were almost taken from their hinges as a third soldier ran out into the street, the backside of his pants torn to ribbons, with Mr Jinx giving chase.

Tumbleweed waved his arms to get the tall man's attention. 'Duck!'

A wiry middle-aged man threw a punch and hit Angelo clean on the jaw. He retaliated with a blow to the man's gut and followed through with a punch to his nose which made a sickly crunching sound. The man stumbled backwards, tripped over a chair and plunged to the floor.

'What the hell's been goin' on here?' Angelo demanded. 'I thought I told you to go buy a wagon – *and* keep a low profile!'

The place was in disarray. Injured bodies were lying all around the room. Smashed tables and chairs were scattered on the floor along with broken bottles. Tom was propped up on the foot rail, holding his bloody nose.

Tumbleweed removed his hat and scratched his head. 'It wus 'em darn soldiers from the fort started it all. That big 'un tried to kick Mr Jinx, and he wus havin' none of it! Tried warnin' the big fool, but he took no heed. One of his friends hit Tom here on the nose, and thun all hell broke loose. Everyone seemed to want to fight. ' Nother one of them thur soldiers wus as crazy as a sheepherder! No tellin' wut he would have done if'n Mr Jinx hadn't stepped in, and chased him clean outta the bar.'

'I hope your friends are goin' to pay for the damage, seeing it was them that started it!' the barkeep said in loud voice.

Angelo frowned. 'The way I see it, I think you'd better take that up with the fort commander. I'm sure those soldiers did their fair share.' He took a fresh twenty-dollar bill from his shirt pocket and placed it on the counter. 'That'll help cover your loss.'

Tom got to his feet and checked himself in the mirror behind the bar. He wiped the fresh blood from his face with his sleeve. 'I swear, if anyone else hits me in the nose, I'm gonna explode!'

'Then I suggest that from here on out you keep it real clean,' growled Angelo.

Evening was drawing in as the three men headed back toward Tumbleweed's shack. Angelo rode alongside Tom, who was driving the newly acquired wagon with a two-horse team. The old man dawdled behind, constantly urging the mule to quicken its pace.

'Hey, big fella, we've trouble a-comin'!' the old man yelled.

Angelo looked over his shoulder. There were a dozen cavalrymen riding at full gallop towards them. 'Let me do the talkin',' he replied quickly, turning to face them.

The troopers reined their mounts to a halt in an uneven line in front of the three men. The forty-year-old captain in charge sat tall in the saddle as he held Angelo's steady gaze with his dark eyes.

'Evening, gentlemen!'

'Anythin' we can help you soldier-boys with?' asked Angelo.

'One of my troopers reckons you had a little set-to back in town with some of my men.'

'What of it?' growled Tom, belligerent as ever.

'I have three men out of action because of it.' He pointed to a trooper to his left. 'This man was lucky; he only received minor injuries to his buttocks. The others were too badly injured to move, so we had to leave them in town.' The officer directed his attention to the animal. 'And there, unless I'm much mistaken, is the culprit. Is he yours, old man?'

'Mr Jinx don't belong to anyone,' said Angelo.

'Then no one will mind me putting him out of his misery,' said the captain, starting to draw his Colt from leather.

Almost faster than the eye could follow, Angelo drew his own six-shooter. 'Let's get one thing clear, Captain, I don't make friends easy, but that dog's the closest thing I've got to one. You pull a gun on him, and it's like you're pullin' it on me. And I don't take too kindly to that. Get the picture?'

The officer moved his hand away from his pistol and turned to Angelo. 'I don't know who you are, mister, but pull a gun on an army officer in these parts and you're in a heap of trouble.'

'Well, we sure don't want any trouble, do we?' Angelo said wryly. 'So if you wouldn't mind clearin' the way, I'd be obliged.'

The captain heeled his horse forward. 'You haven't heard the last of this, mister! There might not be any law as such around these parts, but I'll find a way to see that you all pay for what happened back there.'

The officer and his men headed north for the fort while Angelo, the old man and Tom carried along the eastern trail towards Tumbleweed's shack.

CHAPTER FOUR

As soon as they got back Quincy cleared everything off the small wooden table with a sweep of his arm. 'All right, gather round,' he snapped. 'We all have jobs to do, so listen up.'

The old man grabbed a chair. 'And who put ye in charge?'

'Listen to me, you stupid old goat. I know that fort like the back of my hand and most of the folk who work alongside the military. If we need somethin', I can get it. If we run into trouble, I know who will be able to get us out of it.'

'As long as everyone does as they're told, there shouldn't be any problems,' Angelo pointed out, throwing a meaningful glance at Tom.

Quincy said, 'Angelo, in the mornin' you ride alone to the fort and make yourself known to the CO, Colonel Joshua Winthorpe. We'll give you a head start. By the time we get there, you should've cleared everythin' with him.'

'What's this colonel like?'

'He's easy-goin'. You've nothin' to worry about with him,' Quincy replied. 'But the same can't be said for his adjutant, Captain John Burke. He likes everythin' done strictly by the book. If anythin' looks out of place, he'll be on to it.'

As the night went on Angelo chose to separate himself from the rest of the men. He sat quietly smoking a cigarette on the porch with Mr Jinx lying at his feet. Listening to the sounds of the nightlife and gazing at the moon, he gave a little smile as he remembered the young lady he'd seen in town. The way her eyes sparkled as she spoke to him, the way her full lips had smiled at his embarrassment. Then he went across to the barn and made himself comfortable in an empty stall. He had an early start tomorrow.

Angelo crossed the prairie at an easy pace, and dawn was an hour into the past by the time Fort Concho came into view. It would take another hour to reach the fort gates, which would give him plenty of time to get his story straight. He'd left Mr Jinx behind with the old man, as he wanted nothing to jeopardize his initial meeting with the colonel.

Although he hadn't said much while he was in

their company, he had made a careful study of each of his companions. Apart from Quincy, they all looked as if they couldn't tell skunks from house cats. There was Ryan, a young kid of nineteen. He was of average height and build, with long greasy hair, small grey eyes and buck teeth. Brad Matlock was in his mid-twenties. The first thing that was noticeable about him was his tight red curly hair. It matched his fiery temper, for he was loud-mouthed and aggressive with it. Baby-faced Frank McCall, on the other hand, was the quiet one, but always to be found gently caressing the butt of his six-gun. Finally there was young Jimmy Brown, twenty-one years of age. His wiry frame stood four inches short of six feet. His face was pear-shaped, with beady eyes that were drawn close together.

Fort Concho covered an area of forty acres and consisted of forty buildings which were built from sandstone and pecan wood. There were two sets of gates on the south wall. Angelo took the east gate, which gave access to the officers' and commanding officer's quarters. He was soon challenged by a heavily built sergeant and a trooper carrying a carbine.

'State your name and business!' the sergeant said in husky voice.

'The name's, uh, Grubb,' Angelo said. 'Edward Grubb.' No sooner had the words left his mouth than he wished he could take them back. *Grubb! . . . Who the hell has a name like Grubb?* 'I'm here on government business and need to talk to Colonel Winthorpe.'

'He's at headquarters, far side of the fort.' The sergeant turned to the trooper. 'Take him to the colonel.'

So far so good, Angelo thought. He looked around. There seemed to be plenty going on. Hopefully that meant they could get on with digging for the gold without arousing too much unwanted interest.

Angelo's escort left him outside headquarters, which was situated on the northeastern side of the fort. The tall man dismounted and tied his horse to the hitching post. He dusted himself down and straightened his tie before entering the reception. It was a small, rather plain room containing a two-seater leather couch and a small table and chair by an open fireplace. There was a portrait of George Armstrong Custer hanging from the chimneybreast along with the regimental colors. To the right, a corridor ran the full length of the building, leading to the administration offices, and to the left was the CO's office. A corporal was sifting through paperwork at the desk directly opposite the main door.

The corporal looked up. 'Yes, can I help you?'

'I'm here to see the colonel.'

'Is he expecting you?'

'No, but I'm here on government business and it's important that he knows I'm here.'

The corporal gave Angelo the once over, then said, 'Your name?'

Inwardly Angelo cringed again. 'Edward Grubb.'

'Wait here.'

He went and knocked on the CO's door, then walked in and closed it behind him. A moment later he came back out with the colonel in tow.

Colonel Winthorpe beckoned Angelo with his hand. 'Good day, Mr Grubb. I understand you've come to see me on government business? Please, step inside.'

Angelo entered the CO's office and at the colonel's bidding sat in the chair on the visitor's side of the desk.

Colonel Winthorpe was in his late forties. He was of average build and height, with light-brown hair that was just showing signs of graying at the temples. His bronzed face and hooded eyes told a story of a man who for many years had been used to being exposed to the elements.

'I'm here to do a survey for a new hospital and school,' said Angelo, surprised at just how uncomfortable he was with lying.

Winthorpe's eyes lit up, which only made Angelo feel worse. 'This is amazing news! We've been asking for a new hospital for months now, and as usual we thought that no one had taken any notice.'

'Well, nothin' is set in stone just yet, Colonel – if you'll, uh, pardon the pun. It all depends on the land hereabouts. When we raise buildings, we like to make sure they *stay* raised.'

'Ah, I see. You need to check the land first, make sure you have a stable foundation to build upon.'

'Exactly, sir. There's a lot of underground streams, caves and possibly even sinkholes in these parts, and we don't want the new buildings subsidin', now do we?'

Before the colonel could respond, the door behind Angelo opened wide. The colonel pushed his chair back and stood up. 'Abigail! You'll never guess what, my dear! We're to have a new hospital and school!'

'Oh, that's wonderful news, Father!'

Recognizing the voice, Angelo swung around in his chair and came face to face with the girl he'd encountered, albeit briefly, in Santa Angela. He almost leapt to his feet in order to bow his head in her direction.

'Ma'am.'

'Let me introduce my daughter, Abigail,' said the colonel. 'Abigail, this is Mr Edward Grubb.'

Angelo winced.

'It's a pleasure to meet you, Mr—'

'Please, ma'am. Call me . . . Edward.'

She was dressed much as she had been the day before, which did nothing to dampen his excitement.

'Are you planning on staying long?' she asked.

'Well, at least until I've, uh, drawn out the plans for the new buildings. A few days, is my guess.'

'Well, I'll make arrangements for you to have a pleasant stay while you are here,' said the colonel. 'I'm sure you'll find the officers' quarters to your liking.'

'I don't want to put you to any trouble, Colonel.'

'Ha! Think nothing of it. You are a godsend, my friend; it's the least I can do.'

'And you have come just at the right time!' piped up Abigail. 'We are having a dance at the officers' club tonight.' She gave Angelo a smile. 'Do say you'll come?'

'Well, I'm not quite sure, ma'am. I may have to work late tonight.'

'Fiddlesticks! I'm sure there is nothing that can't wait until tomorrow. Let's say seven o'clock. We'll be expecting you.'

CHAPTER FIVE

Angelo watched as the men unloaded the digging tools. Tumbleweed unhitched the horses and led them to the stables to get feed and water.

Quincy, meanwhile, opened up the map and began to follow the directions. He suddenly stopped about three yards from the colonel's living quarters. 'This is it!' he hissed, then handed a pick and shovel to Brad and Frank. 'You can start diggin' while the rest of us can keep a lookout.'

'How come we get to do the diggin'?' Frank whined.

'Keep it quiet,' said Angelo. 'We got company!'

A trooper came up to the two men, took off his slouch hat and wiped the sweat from his brow with his forearm. 'Which one of you is Grubb?' he asked.

Again Angelo winced. 'That'll be me,' he confessed reluctantly.

'Captain Burke's compliments, sir. He wonders if you'd like to join him in the officers' mess for lunch.'

Angelo gave the trooper a curt nod. 'Tell the captain I'll be along shortly.'

The soldier turned and headed back towards the mess hall.

Quincy scowled. 'Remember what I told you about that man. If he smells that somethin's wrong, he'll be on to us. So you better go and keep him from snoopin' around. Oh, and what in tarnation possessed you to pick a name like Grubb?'

Hacked off by the question, Angelo shook his head, then made his way to the officers' mess. He was greeted by a young lieutenant, who escorted him the final distance to Captain Burke's table.

'Excuse me, Captain. This is Mr Grubb.'

Captain Burke turned around, smiled up at his visitor – and froze. 'You!' he husked.

Burke's surprise was mutual, for Angelo had come face to face with none other than the officer who'd threatened to shoot Mr Jinx the night before.

'So *you*'re the man that the colonel wants to keep sweet.' Burke sneered.

'And you're man he's chosen to nursemaid me,' Angelo replied.

As he took a seat across from the officer, Burke hissed, 'Listen, mister, if I had my way, you'd all be locked up for what you did to my men. Especially those villains you have working for you. I've seen them around town, and here in the fort. I wouldn't trust them an inch. So be very careful, because I'll be keeping a close eye on you all.'

'Hey, big fella! I need to talk to ye.'

The voice came from the far side of the room, where Tumbleweed stood with his hat in hand.

Burke grimaced. 'It looks like one of your men needs you more than I do. Maybe we should just skip lunch.'

Angelo shrugged. 'I kinda lost my appetite anyways.'

He hurried over to the old man. 'What is it? You're supposed to be keepin' an eye on things.'

The old man fidgeted with his hat. 'We got a problem,' he said.

'What kind of problem?'

'The gold,' said Tumbleweed. 'It's not there!'

Mr Jinx started barking excitedly when Angelo approached. Quincy said, 'You can see to him later. I need you to take a look at this first.'

Ryan and Jimmy were standing in the hole, which was around five feet deep. Ryan pointed downward. 'Do you see it?'

Angelo peered inside. 'See what?'

'Nothin', that's what! No boxes, no gold, nothing

save more dirt!'

Tom shook his head. 'I might've known it! That map's a fake!'

'The hell it is!' blustered Tumbleweed. 'Those two bars I got stowed away in my cabin're real enough!'

'Quit it!' snapped Angelo. 'Let's think about this a moment.' He did just that, then said, 'Give me the map.'

Quincy unfolded it and handed it to him. He knelt and laid it out on the dirt. After studying it for a while, he took out the makings and rolled himself a smoke.

'Well?' barked Quincy.

'Charlie Two-Shoes was a clever man,' Angelo replied. 'And he drew up a well-detailed map. It's just a pity we missed it the first time around. It would have saved us from diggin' in the wrong place.'

Quincy and Tom studied the piece of paper. Tumbleweed joined the brothers and gave the map the once-over.

'Missed wut?' the old man grumbled. 'I don't see nuthin' different.'

'There are four symbols of the sun. No one thought to ask why he'd drawn these on the map. Also, there's the figure nine beside the tree.'

Quincy growled impatiently, 'Can we please get

to the point?'

'OK, listen up. The first symbol of the sun is directly above the tree. I reckon that would mean midday. The others more'n likely represent hourly intervals. So I figure at three in the afternoon the tree will cast a shadow, and that's where we start. The nine would have been the height of the tree all those years ago . . . nine feet. So all we do is put a marker on the tree nine feet from the base and when we see the shadow of the marker on the ground, we start from there.'

'Sounds easy enough, young 'un,' Tumbleweed said.

'You'd better be right, big man,' grouched Quincy. "It's already a little after two.'

'OK, so we have a little time to kill.'

'Uh-huh. And we'll all pass it together, while my boys fill in this here hole.'

Angelo gave Mr Jinx a bowl of water and some beef jerky from the wagon, then lay with his back to the tree, which gave him shade from the harsh sunlight. The dog lay quietly next to him, chewing on the jerky.

At three, Angelo showed a thin-lipped smile and said, 'All right, on your feet. It's time!' He took their tape measure and moseyed over to Quincy. 'Give me your knife and squat against the tree. I'll climb up on your shoulders to mark the height.'

From the base of the trunk, Tumbleweed held one end of the measure and handed the other to Angelo, who without warning stood on Quincy's head to get the extra height needed to mark off the nine feet.

'Sonofabitch! You almost took my eye out,' yelled Quincy.

'Stop your whinin', Quince,' Angelo said, then thrust the steel blade into the tree. As it cast its shadow over the ground, the knife marker could clearly be seen.

Quincy handed the old man the map. 'You do it . . . you follow the directions.'

Tumbleweed stood directly above the shadow and began to mumble. 'Left five paces . . . one, two. . . .'

Everyone watched with anticipation as the old man moved in the directions that were marked on the map. He then froze as if his feet had suddenly grown roots.

'Is that it? Is that the place?' Quincy asked.

The old man didn't answer.

'What's wrong, you old fool? Is that the place or not?'

'Wull, not quite.'

'What do you mean?' Tom asked. 'Is it or isn't it?'

'The last turn is ten paces.'

'So walk ten paces, you stupid old goat.'

'I can't!'

Quincy threw down his hat. 'Dagnabit, Tumbleweed. What the hell's wrong?'

'I got ten paces still to walk. To do that I'd need to be able to walk through walls . . . an' thun I'd end up smack inside the colonel's livin' quarters!'

He was right. The directions led directly to a spot inside Colonel Winthorpe's bedroom. Angelo peered through the window and corrected himself. 'Unless the colonel's taken to wearin' women's clothin', my guess is that it's his daughter's bedroom.'

'So where does that leave us?' demanded Quincy.

'I figure an hour ought to do it.'

'Do what?' Quincy barked.

'You'll need at least an hour to get in, dig up the gold and get out again. We'll have to make sure the colonel and his daughter are kept busy.'

'And how the hell do we do that?' asked Tom.

'There's a ball tonight at the officers' mess, and I've been invited. I'll make sure the colonel and his daughter don't get any ideas about leavin' until I know you have the gold safely loaded on the wagon.'

'How will ye know?' Tumbleweed asked.

'Because Quincy here will send word to the officers' mess, saying that my presence is required elsewhere.'

'And ye can trust the sumbitch to do that?'

'Oh, yes. Because I'll be takin' Tom here with me as insurance.'

'What?' Tom bellowed.

'Quincy might be a lot of things,' said Angelo, 'but I doubt that he's low enough to double-cross his own brother.'

Well, that was the plan, anyway.

CHAPTER SIX

As Angelo and Tom entered the mess hall, they were greeted by a corporal in dress uniform. Angelo recognized the man as being the one he'd met on the front desk at headquarters. A look of disapproval shadowed the man's face as he looked the two grubby men up and down.

'The colonel is expecting you, sir, if you'd like to follow me.'

Angelo glanced at Tom and said, 'You stay right here. When Tumbleweed shows up, point him in my direction.'

There were at least two dozen couples on the floor, dancing to the music of the regimental band. A large group of officers looked on, hoping to catch the eye of one of the young ladies. Some of the older couples were sitting in a group. To their right stood a gingham-covered table filled with punch bowls and hors d'oeuvres. There, another group of officers were smoking cigars and drinking whiskey. It was to this table that the corporal led Angelo.

'Glad you could make it, Edward,' said the colonel, immediately filling a glass from the nearest punch-bowl and handing it to him. He put his glass down and pulled out a cigar case. 'Finest Cubans that money can buy, young man,' he said. 'Help yourself.'

Angelo took one from the case, rolled it between his thumb and forefinger, then put it to his nose to take in the aroma. 'Mm, it's been a long time since I've had the pleasure, Colonel.'

As the colonel struck a match and held it towards him, Angelo spotted Abigail entering the room. He froze. She was on the arm of Captain Burke, who appeared only as a faint blur to him. She was elegantly dressed in a flowing midnight-blue velvet evening gown that clung to her curves. A matching ribbon held her brushed-back hair in place, and a cameo brooch choker adorned her slender neck.

Angelo blew out the match and placed the Cuban in his top pocket. Abigail greeted him with a smile and held out one small hand. He bowed slightly and gently kissed it.

Captain Burke raised his eyebrows. 'I must say, I'm taken aback, Grubb. You do have some gentlemanly attributes after all! Maybe there's more to you than meets the eye.'

'You'd be surprised,' Angelo replied briefly.

'Well said, Edward.' Abigail smiled, adding, 'I take it that you have already met our Captain Burke?'

'You could say that I've had the pleasure. Twice, actually.'

Burke frowned. 'Why don't you get the lady a cup of punch while we take this dance?'

Before Angelo could answer, Burke took hold of Abigail's arm and led her on to the dance floor.

The colonel poured himself another cup of punch. 'Well, if you'll excuse me, I think I'll leave you young people alone. I must be seen to mingle, you know.'

'Don't mind me, Colonel. I'll have to be leaving shortly myself. We have an early start tomorrow.'

He glanced toward the main door, where Tom was sitting drinking a cup of punch. He hated deceiving these folks, especially Abigail. But the way he saw it, with the reward money he stood to gain by the recovery of the gold, he could still give them the school and hospital they so desperately needed anyway.

He watched enviously as Captain Burke held Abigail and danced to a slow waltz. After a moment he stepped on to the dance floor, weaved between the other dancers until he reached Abigail and

Burke. He tapped the officer on the shoulder and as he turned to see who it was, Angelo cut in, took Abigail in his arms and waltzed away with her.

Abigail looked softly into Angelo's eyes. 'I think Captain Burke is a little angry at you, and quite frankly I can't blame him!'

'Well, ma'am, I thought this was an "excuse me", so it's not entirely my fault.'

'You intrigue me, Edward!'

'Ma'am?'

'Well, if you'll forgive me for saying, you look more like a saddle tramp than a government official. Some of your noticeable traits could be that of a hired gun. But yet when the need arises, you step up to the mark. And may I also say that you dance rather well.'

Angelo looked over at Tom. The man was gesturing to him. Regretfully he released Abigail and stepped back from her. 'I'm sorry, Miss Abigail, but it seems that I'm wanted elsewhere.'

He was gratified by the look of disappointment that came into her eyes.

Burke wasted little time in seizing his opportunity. He shoved Angelo aside and swept Abigail back into the swirl of dancers. Angelo turned and hurried across to Tom. 'What is it?'

'You'd better come quick,' he said. 'There's been trouble.'

'What kind of trouble?'

Tom turned and hurried out into the night. 'All I know is that it's all gone wrong.'

They crossed the parade ground at a trot, and were quickly swallowed up by the shadows. 'It's all gone wrong,' Tom muttered again as they turned a corner and Angelo saw at once that the wagon was gone – and so were Quincy, Tumbleweed and the others. Only Mr Jinx was still there – and one of them had tied him to the tree before they lit out.

'Wha—?'

Without warning Tom turned on his heel so that Angelo ran straight into him, then he punched Angelo hard in the stomach. 'For you, that is!'

He crowded Angelo fast, giving him no chance to recover, and all the spite he'd been saving up for the man came boiling to the surface in a flurry of punches against which Angelo could do nothing but go down.

He lost count of the number of punches, and when Tom started throwing vicious kicks into the mix, the world he'd known to this point became a world full of hurt. He had no idea when it ended. He was unconscious long before Tom finally stopped.

'You have a lot of explaining to do, mister.'

Angelo awoke with a start. He had been taken

into the headquarters block and thrown roughly on to the two-seater sofa. Captain Burke was towering over him, and in the background Colonel Winthorpe and Abigail were frowning at him. Angelo squeezed his eyes shut against a thumping headache. He felt stiff, achy, thirsty, and nauseous.

'I don't know what the hell you're up to, but I'm going to get to the bottom of it!' Burke continued.

The colonel cut him short. 'Captain Burke!'

Burke stepped aside so that Winthorpe could take center stage. The colonel said, 'What's this all about, Edward? My men find you beaten half to death, your workmen and their wagon have disappeared and my daughter's room has been ransacked and dug up! Just what have you and your friends been up to?'

It was, Angelo thought, a very good question. If only his head would stop pounding long enough for him to form an answer. For just a moment he thought about denying any knowledge, but he knew that wouldn't wash. Besides, he had an honest man's instinctive dislike of subterfuge.

'Gold,' he said softly, and looked away from Abigail before he could see the hurt in her face.

'What?' asked the colonel.

'I'm not a surveyor. I don't work for the government. My name is Angelo, not Edward Grubb. I – we – came here to dig up a cache of Confederate gold that was buried here years ago. Our plan – that is, the old man and me – was to retrieve the gold and then turn it in for the reward. Our so-called "partners" had other ideas.'

'Captain, arrest this man, whoever he is!'

'Hold hard, there, Captain. I know things don't look too good from where you're standing, but believe me when I say that my intentions were honorable.'

'Honorable! You don't know the meaning of the word,' Burke growled.

Angelo got up, swayed a little, and when the room stopped tilting, went over to the corporal's desk. He took a slip of paper from his jacket pocket, helped himself to a pen and then wrote briefly on the reverse side. 'I want you to have this, Colonel,' he said when he was finished.

'What is it?'

'I'd already made up my mind that you were gonna get the school and hospital you want. This is a receipt for ten thousand dollars I just deposited in the Bank of Santa Angela. I've written a note on the back and signed it over to you. If I'm not back within ten days, do what you want with it.'

The colonel looked surprised. 'I don't understand!'

'Look, it's like I said. The old man and me, we were going to hand the gold over to you for the reward. Now they've doubled-crossed me and taken the old man with them, and I'd bet my life he didn't go willingly. Take your men and track down these thieves, sure – but let me go along. My concern is for him. They'll either kill him or leave him out in the middle of the desert to rot.'

'I swear, if this is some sort of trickery. . . .'

'It's not. And with respect, Colonel, time's a-wastin'.'

Winthorpe took the point. 'Captain, prepare C troop to move out at first light. Take enough supplies to last the week. I want those thieves caught and that gold returned, do you understand?'

'Sir!'

As Burke left the room, Angelo looked sheepishly at Abigail. Her expression was almost impossible to read. 'My apologies, Miss Abigail,' he said quietly. 'My part in this isn't anywhere near as bad as it seems.'

The girl turned away and made no reply, and her silence was worse than a slap in the face.

CHAPTER SEVEN

Angelo finished tightening his saddle girth. He'd recovered his gunbelt from his gunny sack and was tying the strap to his leg when Captain Burke rode up to him.

'Just remember, Angelo. This is a military operation, and I'm in command of it. You're just a civilian – and a suspect one, at that. So keep out of my way and do as you're told.'

'Anything you say, Cap'n,' Angelo replied softly.

'Take your place at the back of the column with the wagons.'

The twenty-four troopers rode in single file with two wagons at the rear. Captain Burke and a shavetail lieutenant took point at the head of the column. Ignoring Burke's order, Angelo rode out ahead to scout the trail, with Mr Jinx racing alongside him.

The gold-heavy Randall wagon had left a trail that

headed south along the banks of the River Conchos. They followed it right through the day, and though men and horses both were showing signs of fatigue by late afternoon, Burke wouldn't let up the pace.

Angelo finally dropped back to ride alongside the captain. 'I suggest you camp in yonder gorge,' he said. 'It's got good cover.'

Burke frowned. 'I'll decide where and when to rest, mister.'

'Then you'll know it's best to find your campsite before full dark hits. Besides which, if you don't rest these animals soon, you'll end up walkin' the rest of the way.'

Captain Burke raised his hand. 'Ho! Lieutenant, I think we'll camp over there among those rocks for the night.'

Angelo raised his eyebrows.

'Why the surprised look?' Burke asked. 'I was just about to give the order to camp for the night anyway, before you cut in.'

Angelo found himself a spot with good cover away from the soldiers. He sat with his back against the rockface with Mr Jinx at his feet keeping watch. After rolling a smoke, he lit it from the small fire that he'd made to keep out the night chill. The young lieutenant strolled over carrying two plates of food.

'Thought you and your dog might like some grub.' He handed a plate to Angelo and put the other next to Mr Jinx. 'It's not much . . . what passes for beef stew out here. But it's wholesome.'

'Thanks.'

'My name is Robert Feathersham. I believe everyone already knows who you are.'

Angelo glanced down at Mr Jinx and then smiled. 'Funny, that,' he said.

'What is?'

'I do believe you're the first person besides me that he hasn't growled at.'

The lieutenant crouched and gave Mr Jinx a rub behind the ears. 'I love dogs. I guess he can sense that I mean him no harm. Tell me something, though, Angelo. These men we're chasing. Are they as dangerous as they say?'

'The Randalls are nothin' more than opportunists and petty thieves. But gold can change a man. An' there ain't much that's more dangerous than a desperate man with gold fever. How old are you, kid?'

'Twenty, sir.'

'Fresh out of the Point, no doubt.'

'Yes, sir.'

'Been out here long?'

'Two weeks.'

'Seen any action?'

'Nope.'

'Well,' Angelo assured him, 'be patient, Lieutenant. You will. And soon!'

The night passed without incident and at first light C Troop was ready to push on. Captain Burke and Lieutenant Feathersham were busy studying a map as Angelo crossed over to them.

'They're heading for the Mexican border, I'm sure of it,' Burke was saying to Feathersham. 'We'll keep heading south.'

'You're wrong, Cap'n,' said Angelo. 'My guess is that they'll turn and head back along the Goodnight-Lovin' trail. They're probably goin' to cross the border into New Mexico. If that's so, then they have two choices – keep on the cattle trail or go into El Paso. But I figure they'll follow the cattle trail, as the canyon will give more cover from the elements and anythin' else they might run into.'

Burke took off his hat and wiped the sweat from his forehead with his sleeve. 'I don't remember asking for your opinion, mister.'

'Well, you've got it anyway. And it's not just an opinion, Cap'n. My gut tells me it's a cast-iron certainty.'

'He might be right, sir,' said Feathersham.

'No, we'll keep on going south. Lieutenant, prepare the men to move out.'

*

Disgruntled muttering could be heard from some of the troopers as Burke led them further south into the badlands of Texas towards Del Rio and the Rio Grande. They were out in the open, and away from cover of the gorge that ran along the Conchos River. It was way past noon, it had been a long, hot and demanding ride, and once again Burke showed no indication of calling a halt any time soon.

The rugged terrain slowed progress still further. On the high ground up ahead there were any number of rock formations which would be an ideal place to take a few hours' rest.

Suddenly Lieutenant Feathersham reined his horse to a halt. 'We've got company! There, up on the ridge to the left . . . smoke. See it?'

'I see it,' murmured Angelo.

'What do you reckon?' Feathersham asked.

'Well, I'd rule out a welcomin' committee.'

Captain Burke took a pair of binoculars from his saddle-bags and focused on the top of the ridge. 'I can't see a damn thing. Except for the smoke, everything looks fine.'

'Well, I suggest we proceed with caution,' suggested Angelo.

'We can do better than that. Lieutenant, send one of the men to check it out.'

'Not a wise move, Cap'n.'

Burke glared at Angelo. 'I'll decide what's wise and what isn't.'

Lieutenant Feathersham cut one of the troopers from the column and sent him to investigate the trail of smoke that climbed into the clear blue sky. Angelo watched as the trooper rode out of sight. A few moments later, a single gunshot filled the air.

Burke gently spurred his horse into a walk. 'Bring six men, Lieutenant, and follow me.'

Angelo pulled his Winchester from its boot and followed the troopers as they moved off. They made their way up the slope to the top of the ridge. The sight that greeted them made the young lieutenant turn his head and shudder.

Angelo surveyed the immediate area for signs of danger. 'You satisfied now, Cap'n?' he asked as he slid the rifle back into its boot.

There were telltale signs of dry shrubbery around the small fire which had been used to produce the white smoke that first got their attention. The trooper who had been sent to scout ahead lay face down with three arrows in his back. His horse was missing, along with the cartridge belt, carbine and sidearm. Close by lay the naked body of one of the outlaws. He was spread-eagled face up and secured with rawhide thongs staked to the ground by narrow wooden poles. His eyes had been gouged out and were lying in the dirt next to his tongue and ears.

Deep knife cuts covered the torso and face where scores of fire ants feasted on the honey that had been poured into them. The ruthless sun had blistered his whole body. Hot coals from the fire had been placed between his legs.

'Dear God, who could have done this? Comancheros?'

'No . . . Apaches, and not your every day Apache, neither. These are Chiricahua,' said Angelo. 'The best of the best.'

'How the hell do you figure that one out, mister? There are no hostiles in this area.'

'Well, there are now. They've left their callin' card!' Angelo pointed to an arrow stuck in the ground with a colored sash tied to it. 'See that? Every Chiricahua carries a sacred arrow and a sash. He uses it to show that he'll stand his ground and fight to the death. This is a message for you, Cap'n. I figure they want our horses and guns.'

'Ha! I don't think a few Apaches are going to be much of a problem, if they *are* Apaches!'

'You carry on along this trail, fella, and you're gonna to find out and lead everyone to their deaths in the process. Now, you can do what the hell you like, but I'm headin' west to catch up with whatever's left of the Randalls.'

Burke dismounted and looked closely at the mutilated body of the man staked to the ground, then he turned to face Angelo. 'Who was he?'

'If it wasn't for that mop of red hair, his own mother wouldn't recognize him. That was Brad Matlock.'

Mr Jinx ran up the slope, barking excitedly. Angelo asked, 'What's up, fella?'

A trooper yelled, 'Rider coming in fast, sir!'

Up on the high ridge heading towards them at full gallop was a rider low in the saddle. He was being pursued by four Apache warriors on horseback.

Angelo swung his horse around. 'Cover me!' he yelled as he heeled the gelding hard in the flanks, and the animal took off at full speed with Mr Jinx at its side.

As he drew closer to the Indians Angelo drew his Colt and fired it at the lead Apache. The bullet missed the rider but tore through the horse's shoulder. Its forelegs buckled and it went down head first, throwing its rider into the dirt. The Apache quickly recovered from the fall and returned fire with a Spencer carbine, using the dead horse for cover.

The lone rider was almost level with Angelo when suddenly his horse stumbled, incapable of maintaining the speed the rider demanded. The animal came to an abrupt halt and he was thrown over the horse's head. A cloud of dust exploded as he thudded to the ground.

Angelo yelled out as he passed him, 'Keep down, don't move!' The rider did as he was told.

Mr Jinx leapt over the dead horse just as the Apache struggled to reload the carbine. The dog locked on to his arm, tearing through muscle and bone.

Angelo, meanwhile, emptied his Colt at the remaining warriors. The Apache to his far left yelled out his death cry as a bullet tunneled through his throat and exited in a rush of blood at the back of his neck.

As the last two rode parallel, one of them took aim with a bow while the other raised his lance in the air. There was only forty feet between them; Angelo sensed the danger of being caught in the middle and quickly reined his gelding to a halt. He tore his Winchester from its boot, levered and squeezed the trigger, but not before the Apache released his bowstring.

The bullet drilled through the Apache's temple. The arrow skimmed the surface of Angelo's thigh, leaving a shallow groove. The gelding reared up on its hind legs, its belly facing the oncoming Apache. As it came back down on all fours, Angelo fired the rifle a second time. The bullet penetrated the top of the horse's head, throwing bone and tissue into its rider's face. The lance fell from his grip and he toppled back over the horse's croup and into the dirt.

Saliva dripping from his bared fangs, Mr Jinx was quick to follow through, attacking the warrior. It didn't take the dog long to finish him.

Angelo reined the gelding to a halt, took his canteen and poured water on the wound, then used his kerchief as a makeshift bandage. Mr Jinx wandered over to him, his snout and paws covered in blood.

'OK, feller,' Angelo said, dry-mouthed from the recent action. 'Let's go see to this greenhorn, then we can get cleaned up.'

Now that the danger was over the rider had recovered his horse and was adjusting the girth. From the back, his build looked more like that of a young skinny kid. He was dressed in a fancy buckskin jacket and tight-fitting pants to match, and wore a large-brimmed, low-crowned hat.

'You all right, friend?' Angelo called as he closed the last few yards.

The rider took off the hat, allowing the long hair that had been tucked inside to flow freely on to her shoulders, as she turned and gazed into Angelo's eyes.

'You!' he breathed in disbelief. 'What in tarnation are *you* doing here?'

'I thought you'd be pleased to see me,' said Abigail.

Then she fainted.

CHAPTER EIGHT

Angelo dismounted, scooped Abigail into his arms and carried her back down to the waiting column. He stretched her out in wagon-shade and then spilled some water between her lips. She coughed and came back to consciousness.

'Good grief, girl!' blustered Burke. 'Have you lost your mind? What on earth are you doing out here?'

She fixed Angelo with a look, then turned her attention to Burke. 'I needed to find out something,' she said. 'This man Angelo . . . I made the mistake of taking him at face value, and I was hurt – deeply hurt, Angelo – when he proved to be a complete fraud. However, I have a Christian nature. I'd give anyone the benefit of the doubt.'

'So you came out here to see for yourself whether or not I was still here or had left to join up with my "partners-in-crime",' Angelo finished.

She nodded.

'Well,' he said, 'as you can see, I'm still here. And a good thing for you that I am. Now, I think we'd better get the heck out of here, Cap'n.'

Burke frowned. 'You think they'll be back?'

'You'd better believe it. 'Fact, I'd say they're watchin' us right now, plannin' their next move.'

The column turned west and headed for the cattle trail. Because it was too risky to send her back to the fort, Abigail rode in the chuck wagon alongside the driver, with Mr Jinx resting in back. They were traveling over open ground, which made them vulnerable to any prying Apache eyes. Angelo knew it would take at least another day to reach the Pecos, which meant spending one night on the prairie.

It was almost sundown when Captain Burke ordered the troop to dismount and take up defensive positions, while the appointed cook prepared a meal and fresh coffee. At Abigail's insistence, Angelo hopped up on to the tailgate and allowed her to clean and bind his leg wound.

Mr Jinx got up and wagged his tail as Lieutenant Feathersham approached. He crouched and gave the dog a rub behind the ears. 'How's the leg?' he asked Angelo.

'Couple of days from now it'll be as good as new.'

After supper, Burke drew up a roster for guard

duty. He placed six men in a small perimeter close to the wagons. Angelo had cleared a place for Abigail's bed on the floor of the chuck wagon, while he bedded down underneath. He took out the makings and rolled himself a cigarette. After lighting it, he lay with his head resting on his saddle and smiled at the thought of her sleeping so close to him.

The clatter of pots and pans being thrown into the storage drawers of the chuck wagon woke Angelo from his sleep. The camp was in disarray, with men yelling and shouting as they ran in all directions with horse tack and their bedding. Abigail climbed down from the wagon.

'What's going on?' she asked Angelo.

He shook his head, stood and put on his gun-belt, then grabbed his hat and headed for the supply wagon, where Lieutenant Feathersham was fastening the back curtain. 'Somethin' I should know?'

The lieutenant looked over his shoulder. 'Two of the men had their throats cut while they slept. No one saw or heard a thing. Captain Burke is furious.'

Just then a middle-aged sergeant hurried over to them. 'Compliments of Captain Burke, sir. He says to move out and he'll catch up.'

'Where is the captain, anyway?' Feathersham asked.

'He took a handful of troopers out to see if he could find the Apaches that got into camp last night.'

'Thank you, Sergeant. Have the men ready to move out in ten minutes.' He looked anxiously at Angelo. 'It's going from bad to worse, isn't it?'

'Look on the bright side, Lieutenant. There's always the chance that Burke might get lost.'

As the wheels of the supply wagon rolled over the hard dry trail, the driver fastened his kerchief over his nose and mouth to eliminate the foul stench coming from the corpses he was hauling.

Once more they came to a halt. Angelo heeled his horse and rode to the head of the column. 'What's up, Lieutenant?'

'I'm not sure, but it looks like a wagon about a mile up ahead.'

Angelo narrowed his eyes and searched the terrain. 'Yeah, I see it. I'll go take a closer look.'

Mr Jinx jumped around excitedly. 'Stay boy. No need for us both to go, I'll be back before you know it.'

He heeled the gelding into a lope and pulled the Winchester from its boot. It didn't take him long to reach the covered wagon. There was no sign of anyone or the team of horses. He slowly circled around it, reined the gelding and slid from the saddle.

Suddenly he heard snoring coming from inside. He cautiously pulled back the curtain to reveal a familiar face. He climbed over the tailgate and prodded the old man with the barrel of his rifle.

'Get up! This is no time to be sleepin'.'

Tumbleweed sat up. 'Huh? Sumbitch . . . you! Whure the hell have ye bin, young 'un? I'd almost given up on ye.'

'Well it sure is good to see you, too, old man.'

'Are ye alone?'

'No, old-timer, I've got some soldier-boys with me.'

'Darn soldiers. Ye knows how much I detest 'em.'

'You might be glad of 'em before this is over.'

'As long as that sumbitch we met on the road to my place ain't one of 'em.'

Angelo bit his bottom lip. 'Well—'

'Doggone it, Angelo. I thought things wur lookin' up. That piece of horse dung's so mean, he'd steal a fly from a blind spider.'

'Maybe he would. But right now we got bigger things to worry about.'

'Such as?'

'Apaches.'

The sound of approaching horses prompted Angelo to pull back the curtain just enough to catch a glimpse of Captain Burke and six troopers reining their mounts to a halt.

Angelo turned to the old man. 'Damn!'

'Wut's up?'

'Nothin' for you to worry about, old man. You stay here until I tell you to come out. Got it?'

'Sure! Get a wiggle on, my throat's parched. Feels like the backside of a 'coon's butt.'

'I'll be as quick as I can.'

Six carbines were trained on him as he climbed from the wagon.

'Whoa there, boys. A man can get the wrong idea when you're pointin' guns at him. Could save us all a whole lot of trouble if you put 'em up.'

Burke leaned forward. 'I assume this is the wagon the outlaws used to carry off the gold?'

'Yup.'

'I heard voices coming from inside. Who else is in there?'

'Just the old man.'

Burke turned to his men. 'If he comes out carrying a weapon, blast him.'

'Come on out, Tumbleweed, and keep your hands where everyone can see 'em.'

The old man slowly climbed down and strolled over to Angelo's horse. Moving his gaze toward Burke, he said, 'Ye don't mind if'n I get myself a swig of water, do ye?'

'Make it quick. Angelo, relieve the prisoner of his gun. He can double up with you till we join the rest of the troop.'

'Now just wait a doggone minute, Cap'n. I ain't no outlaw!'

'You made off with gold that didn't belong to you. In my eyes, that makes you as guilty as the rest of those rogues.'

The old man took off his hat and slapped his thigh with it. 'Is that a bluff, or do ye mean it for real play?'

'He was taken against his will, Burke, and well you know it,' snapped Angelo. 'Besides, you might just have need of his gun if we run into those Apaches again.'

Burke made an angry sound in his throat. 'Just get him back to the column! Right now we're sitting targets out here!'

CHAPTER NINE

Abigail and Lieutenant Feathersham were waiting by the chuck wagon as the captain and the others approached.

Tumbleweed tapped Angelo on the shoulder. 'Wut in tarnation is she doin' way out here?'

'She wants to make sure I really am one of the good guys.'

Angelo brought the gelding to a halt and the old man slid from the horse and stretched. The lieutenant looked Tumbleweed up and down with a puzzled frown.

'Wut ye gawkin' at?' the old man asked.

Before the lieutenant could answer, an excited bark came from under the wagon as Mr Jinx ran out to greet Angelo.

'Wull, cut off my legs an call me Shorty, if it ain't Mr Jinx,' Tumbleweed said with a gleam in his eye.

The dog greeted the old man, yapping excitedly and wagging his tail. Tumbleweed crouched and rubbed the dog's ears. 'Ye still lookin' after the big fella?'

Mr Jinx responded with a loud bark.

They reached the banks of the River Pecos early afternoon. The trail ran northwards on a slight down-slope with a sheer rock escarpment rising to about forty feet or so, which broadened into an open hillside littered with large rocks. It was perfect ambush country. The troop headed along the gorge, which gave them ample cover from the sun. Tumbleweed and Mr Jinx were riding in the chuck wagon while Abigail rode her mare alongside Angelo at the rear of the column.

After a while Lieutenant Feathersham joined them. 'Has the old man had a chance to tell you yet why he and the wagon were abandoned by the Randall brothers?'

'Not yet, Lieutenant. I'm sure he'll tell us when he's good and ready.'

Feathersham looked concerned. 'I think the captain is expecting a full account when we—'

'*Up ahead!*' a trooper yelled.

About 1,000 yards in front there seemed to be what looked like a dead horse with several buzzards feasting on its carcass. A corporal took off to investigate. The birds were so intent on eating their fill that they hardly noticed the soldier as he hastily brought the mount to a halt.

'Git out the way, you sonsofbitches!' he hollered.

The large birds flapped their wings but made no attempt to abandon their meal. The corporal undid the flap on his holster and removed his pistol, pointed it skyward and fired two shots. They were finally persuaded to take flight.

Angelo turned to the lieutenant. 'The damn fool! If the Apaches didn't know we were here before, they do now!'

The corporal stood in the stirrups. 'Looks like one of ours, Capt—'

His voice cut off as a bullet drilled him through the neck.

'*Take cover*!' yelled Burke.

Angelo pulled the Winchester from its boot and leapt from the saddle. He steadied Abigail's skittish mare while she quickly dismounted and grabbed hold of his hand. Then they ran for cover behind the chuck wagon, where Tumbleweed was grousing.

'Wut in tarnation's goin' on now? Can't a man get any sleep around here?'

'Shut up, old man, and stay low. We have ourselves a sharpshooter.'

The designated horse-handlers had gathered the mounts and dragged them towards the cover of some rocks while their riders found defensive positions. The driver of the chuck wagon sat aboard his high seat, uncertain whether to leave the vehicle or stay where he was in case he needed to make a run for it.

'See anything?' Burke asked in a low voice.

No one answered, and then the sound of a second shot echoed through the air.

With a scream, one of the troopers taking cover by the water's edge pitched over.

'He's way up on that ledge to the left of us, sir!' someone shouted.

'Do you think it's Apaches?' asked Abigail.

'Could be . . . or the Randalls. Either way, they've got the edge on us.'

Captain Burke ordered the men to fire on the ledge.

'You damn fool!' Angelo yelled. 'You're wasting ammunition, and that's just what they want!'

Burke broke cover and ran towards the chuck wagon. Another shot rang out from the top of the ridge, the bullet dug deep into the dirt just a few inches in front of him. He threw himself behind the wagon, landing at Angelo's feet.

'Damn your eyes, Angelo! You question everything I say! But can you do any better?'

'Well, if it was me wearin' those shoulder-bars, I'd sit this one out. We can't go forward an' we can't go back. An' right now we ain't got anythin' to shoot at.

But after dark. . . .'

'Yes?' said Burke, despite himself.

'After dark he won't have anything left to shoot at, either.'

Burke considered that for a moment, then said, 'My own reasoning exactly.'

'I thought it might be.'

Burke turned away and yelled, 'Cease firing! Has anyone been hit apart from Murphy over there?'

'Don't think so, sir,' yelled the non-com.

'Then make the men comfortable. We're sitting tight until dark.'

There were disgruntled mutterings from behind a mound where several troopers, and Feathersham, had taken cover. They had been sitting quietly for over two hours now and the tension among them was becoming apparent.

'Keep the noise down over there, Lieutenant,' Burke hissed.

Angelo decided to chance moving out into the open to get a better view of the sharpshooter's position. He picked up his Winchester and ran to Murphy's dead body, then propped him into a sitting position, using him as a shield. He shaded his eyes from the sun's glare, and scoured the skyline for movement. There was nothing. The area looked quiet.

'I think it's safe to come out now. Looks like whoever was up there has gone.'

'You sure?' Burke asked.

'Yeah, I'm sure.'

The men remounted and the body of Murphy was thrown in the back of the supply wagon. They moved off at a steady pace with two troopers scouting a mile ahead of the column. Tumbleweed complained about riding with a wagon full of corpses. The driver adjusted his neckerchief covering his nose and mouth. 'Tell you what, old man,' he snarled. 'I don't know which is worse, the smell from these here dead men, or the stink comin' from you!'

A full moon dominated the cloudless night sky as the troop stopped to rest beside the thin ribbon of a stream. Angelo took hold of his gelding's reins and led him towards the water's edge to drink. Abigail followed suit.

'You all right?' he asked.

'Sure,' she replied.

He looked at her in the moonlight and smiled. She caught the flash of his teeth and said, 'What?'

'Nothin'.'

'So you just grin like a village idiot for no good reason, is that it?'

'Well, if you must know, I was just . . . admiring you. Your grit. I mean, here you are, out in the middle of nowhere, Apaches breathin' down our necks, and do you complain about it? Not one bit.'

'Why, thank you, kind sir. But maybe you're overlooking the one reason I'm not complaining.'

'Which is. . . ?'

'Because I'm here with you,' she said softly.

Hearing that, he grabbed her tiny waist and pulled her towards him. Her eyes softened as she gazed into his, and closed when his lips gently touched hers.

The softest scuff of boot-leather distracted him.

'Sorry to bother you, Angelo,' the lieutenant interrupted. 'But. . . .'

Angelo pulled away from what was almost but not quite a kiss. 'What is it?' he asked as Abigail concentrated on watering her horse.

The lieutenant blushed to the ears. 'I'm sorry, I didn't mean to, uh . . . I mean, I had no—'

'Forget it,' sighed Angelo. 'What do you want?'

'The captain has decided to make camp for the night. Just thought you ought to know, so that you can see to your horse and find yourself a good spot to bed down.'

CHAPTER TEN

Angelo carried his saddle towards the chuck wagon, where the cook was preparing a meal. Mr Jinx was gnawing on a bone next to Tumbleweed, who was sitting by the fire he'd prepared, stirring what looked like a thick stew in a large skillet borrowed from the cook's supplies. He took a wooden ladle, scooped up some of the liquid, and took a sip.

Angelo drew in the aroma. 'It sure smells good.'

'Sit ye down, it'll be ready in a few minutes.'

Angelo felt the old man watching him covertly. At length Tumbleweed said, 'Yer moonin' after that gal, ain't ye? I can tell. Wull, it ain't healthy.'

'Quit your gripin', old man, and tell me somethin' I don't know!'

After the meal, Angelo lay back and rested his head on his saddle. He took out the makings, rolled a cigarette and lit it with a glowing twig from the fire.

He gazed at the stars in the clear night sky. As he exhaled the smoke, he got to thinking that if it hadn't been for the old man, he would have been well on his way to Tombstone by now. But just like Mr Jinx, Tumbleweed seemed to be in need of a friend. And if the truth be told, he'd become quite attached to the pair of them.

At first light, Angelo kicked Tumbleweed awake.

'Eh? Wut in tarnation are ye up so early fer?'

'I'm going to ride with one of the scouts for a day or two.'

He swung aboard the gelding and allowed the animal to pick its way through camp, until Captain Burke suddenly appeared in his path. 'I hear you are going to do a little scouting,' he said.

'What of it?'

'Nothing. It's probably a wise decision under the circumstances.'

'Oh?'

'Yes. Last night I couldn't help but notice you with Miss Abigail down by the river. You would be well advised to remember that she is a lady, and not one of the dollar whores you're probably used to. Just remember your place, and keep well away. She doesn't need some low-down saddle tramp taking advantage of her. Do I make myself clear?'

Angelo spat off to one side. 'I've got six ways of dyin' sittin' low on my hip, and you've given me cause to use every one of 'em, Burke. But I ain't gonna let you rile me, fella. Leastways not today.'

Burke's top lip twitched nervously as he stalked off to join the burial detail.

'I wouldn't pay too much attention to him, Angelo.'

Angelo hipped around just as Feathersham came out of the slowly retreating shadows. 'It's just his way.'

'He should have stayed at the fort, pushin' his pen. He's not cut out for leadin' men.'

The lieutenant pointed at two mounted men a hundred yards or so upriver. 'Those two will be scouting today. You decide who you want to go with.'

Angelo gave a short, sharp whistle and Mr Jinx came trotting over to him, wagging his tail. 'Ridin in the wagon has put a few pounds on you, boy. Runnin' around with me for a couple of days will soon get rid of it.' He looked toward the top of the gorge. 'Which one will be ridin' up there?'

'That'll be Sergeant Hogan. Trooper Scott will be taking point.'

'OK, I'll ride with Hogan,' Angelo said, heeling the horse into a walk. He gave a curt nod as he neared the soldier. 'You ready?'

'Ready as I'll ever be.'

Hogan was a big man, three inches taller than

Angelo, and he weighed close to 200 pounds, mostly muscle. They ascended the hill at a slow, cautious walk, their eyes everywhere at once. It was slow going, and the gelding stumbled once and almost took a tumble. 'Easy there, big fella, we're almost there,' said Angelo, gently stroking the neck of the skittish horse.

At last they reached the summit. The ground was covered in shrubs and clusters of broom-weed. They had a good all-round view of the area, which showed no signs of danger. Hogan dismounted and crouched to better inspect the ground.

'What is it?' asked Angelo.

'Hoof prints . . . unshod ponies, 'bout six of 'em.'

'Which way are they headed?'

Climbing back into the saddle, Hogan said, 'Looks like they're headin' for the hills to the east of us. Probably miles away, by now.'

Angelo moved to the edge of the gorge, and could see that C Troop was on the move again.

They kept at a slow pace, always keeping a couple of miles between them and the column. At noon, the column stopped to rest.

Hogan reined his horse to a halt and turned to Angelo. 'Looks like the cap'n's takin' a break. We might as well make the most of it. If you can collect some wood from that thicket over there, I'll prepare us a pot of the best coffee you've ever tasted.'

Angelo made a small fire next to a clump of rocks which gave them ample protection from the midday sun.

While the coffee was brewing, Hogan added a generous amount of Scotch whisky. 'Give it another minute, and it'll be perfect. Lessen you're Temperance, that is?'

Angelo sat two tin cups by the fire. 'The way I feel right now, fella, I could drink the full pot all by myself.'

'That's what I like to hear,' Hogan said as he wrapped his kerchief around his hand, lifted the coffee from the fire and poured. 'There's sweetenin' in my sack if you want it.'

'No, it's fine the way it—'

Angelo was cut short by the sound of a rifle being levered. Mr Jinx jumped up and growled.

A young Apache came from behind the rocks carrying a Henry rifle braced against his hip. Angelo figured that, with the warrior's finger clearly on the trigger, it would be foolish to make a move on him.

The Apache's small frame wavered slightly as he turned the rifle on the dog. Angelo quickly grabbed Mr Jinx around the neck. 'Easy, boy. It's OK.'

The warrior looked to be in his late teens. His dark eyes showed no emotion as he turned the rifle back towards the two men and mumbled something in his native tongue.

Hogan turned to Angelo. 'You speak Chiricahua?'

'Nope. But I think it's obvious he wants us to lose our hardware.'

Without saying another word, both men loosened their gunbelts and let them slip to the dirt.

Angelo looked at the buck and wondered where he'd come from and what he was doing way out here all by himself. It was then that Mr Jinx started growling, and Hogan suddenly stiffened. 'He's brought company!'

Angelo followed the line of his companion's gaze and cussed. They were being watched by fifteen mounted Chiricahua Apache warriors who had appeared as if out of nowhere.

It was hard to remain calm, but Angelo knew better than to show the gut-tightening fear he was feeling. The Apaches would take it as a sign of weakness and punish it accordingly.

A warrior at the center of the line moved his pony forward. It was then that Angelo noticed that the Apache was doubled up with a dark-haired woman. When the Apache was level with Angelo and Hogan, he brought his pony to a halt and the woman slipped from the mount. She was about thirty or so, her dark skin and facial features suggesting Mexican heritage. She glared at the two white men.

'I'm Camila, Ulzana's woman. I also translate for him.'

Hogan spat grimly. 'Ulzana. Yeah, I've heard of that sonofabitch. He's nothin' more than a jumped-up renegade Injun, with a handful of followers.'

Camila forced a smile. 'I'd watch my tongue if I was you, soldier blue. It would be easy for my man to pluck it from your mouth.'

Before Hogan could reply, Angelo cut in, 'She's right. That kinda talk could get us both killed, soldier, so button it!'

'What do ya mean . . . *could* get us killed?'

'If he wanted us dead, he would have done it already.'

'Enough!' Camila yelled and then began conversing with the young Apache in Chiricahua. She returned her gaze to Angelo and said, 'Ulzana respects you. He saw you and your wolf kill four of his warriors while the soldier blue cowards stood by and did nothing.'

'Wolf?'

'Your dog look like wolf, and a white wolf is strong medicine to the Chiricahua.'

'What else?'

Camila conversed once more with the Apache leader. His tone seemed to suggest that he was getting a little irritated. 'Ulzana say he has the four gringos and the gold you seek. He say he will trade them for the new rifles and ammunition you are carrying in the wagons.'

Angelo was taken aback. 'Rifles? What rifles?'

Camila frowned. 'Don' play games, *señor.* The rifles that the gringo Quincy told us about.'

'Tell Ulzana there *are* no rifles. The man called Quincy lied to him.'

His answer didn't seem to go down well with Ulzana. He dismounted and walked up to Angelo. His nut-brown skin was smooth and flawless. His long black hair was partially covered by a red bandanna. He was a head shorter than Angelo and the only clothing he wore was a loincloth and high-top moccasin boots.

He began talking again, but this time in broken English. 'The white eyes, Randall, told me that the bluecoats have many new rifles. So why you say different?'

'The Randall brothers would've told you anythin' to avoid a fight.'

Ulzana appeared to be deep in thought for a moment. Then he said, 'We will get the truth from the bluecoat chief. If your words are twisted like a snake, I will know soon enough.'

'You want to talk with Burke? What do you think you can you achieve by that?'

'I will make deal with him. You can lead us safely into the bluecoat camp.'

Angelo thought fast. He assumed that Ulzana had many more warriors hidden. He looked at the array of weapons they were carrying, and noticed that several had rifles that were old and ill-kept. The only decent weapons on display was the Henry repeater that the young Apache had used when the two men were taken by surprise, and the one in Ulzana's hands, and they were probably short on ammunition for these.

'We will ride under a white flag and talk to this man, Burke.'

'Not a good idea, chief. There will be no deal. Burke isn't the kind of man you can talk to. He won't listen.'

Ulzana smiled. 'You are wrong. When he sees the gold and the white-eyes that he is hunting, then he will trade.'

The young Apache leader made a hand gesture to one of his mounted braves. 'Now *you* will see.' The warrior turned his mount and rode back down the trail, then out of sight. He returned moments later with one of the prisoners. Angelo immediately recognized him, it was Quincy Randall. He was tied at the wrists and stagger-stumbling along behind the Apache leading him towards the others.

He spat as he caught sight of Angelo, then cussed, 'Sonofabitch!'

The warrior yanked on the rope forcing Quincy to his knees. He clenched his teeth and glared at his captor, then back to Angelo. 'I swear, if he . . . does that one more time, I'm gonna . . . wrap this rope around his scrawny . . . red neck and choke the life out of him.'

Angelo walked a little closer, and then looked down at Quincy with contempt. 'Where're the others?' he asked.

'If you . . . mean Tom and the . . . boys . . . they're b-back there a-ways. Except for Brad, that . . . is.'

Angelo grimaced. 'Yeah, we saw what they did to Brad.'

'Well then, you could . . . say we have us a . . . situation, big fella. It'll be interestin' to see what happens next,' husked Quincy.

Angelo turned his attention back to Ulzana. 'OK, we'll try this your way. But let me tell you somethin', chief. The cap'n's the kind of man who'll shoot first and ask questions later, if he bothers to ask 'em at all – even if you are carrying a white flag.'

He and Hogan remounted and turned toward C Troop. 'Get the rest of captives ready to move out along with the gold, and follow me. Stay well back,' Angelo told Ulzana. 'But close enough so that the cap'n can see at first glance, you've got what he wants.'

CHAPTER ELEVEN

When C Troop came into view Angelo saw that they had already taken up defensive positions with their backs against a large rock formation. The wagons were being used as barricades with the horses and men safely behind them.

Ulzana brought his group to a halt. 'You go now. Talk with white chief. *Dále'é Sháa*.'

Angelo glanced at Camila for a translation. '*Dále é Sháa* mean you have until the sun rises in the sky again. At first light, Ulzana wants an answer.'

The young chief drew up alongside Angelo and held out an arrow. 'Take this as sign that my words are straight. Hand it to bluecoat chief and tell him, give us what we want, and we can go our ways without bloodshed.'

Angelo took the arrow and nodded as he heeled the horse forward, Hogan riding right alongside him.

He was grim-faced as he rode the grey gelding to within a couple of hundred yards of the barricade; not because of the thought of having to deal with Captain Burke, but because Abigail was caught up in this dangerous mess and there would be no way to guarantee her safety.

Burke, Feathersham, Tumbleweed and Abigail hurried forward to greet them. When he was level, he reined to a halt and dismounted.

'What's happening?' Burke demanded. 'Those are Apaches out there!'

'Yup,' said Angelo. 'And they've got the men and gold we've been after. We can have 'em, too – for a price.'

'I don't cut deals with Indians.'

'I've already told 'em that. But if we don't give 'em what they want, we can kiss the gold goodbye.'

'What are their terms?'

'Simple enough. They want rifles and ammunition.'

Burke laughed. 'Are they crazy? Do they really expect me to hand over our guns to them?'

'Yes, they really do.' He produced the arrow that was tucked inside his rifle boot and handed it to Burke. 'He gives you this as a sign that his words are straight and true. If you give him what he wants, he'll let us to go home in peace.'

Burke took the arrow and gazed at it for a

moment, then threw it to the ground. 'And we're supposed to trust his word?'

'It looks to me as if we don't have much choice, Captain,' said Feathersham.

Burke flicked him a contemptuous glare. 'I'm not going to give in to some jumped-up Apache buck. You got that, Lieutenant?'

'That jumped-up Apache buck, as you call him, can wipe us out at the blink of an eye,' said Angelo. 'He's got enough men to do it, too. I counted fifty, at least. You've got till daybreak to come up with somethin'.'

He brushed past the captain and Abigail followed him. 'Why are you ignoring me?' she asked. 'Have I done something to offend you?'

'Best if you keep your distance, ma'am. That way it will keep my feelin's from—'

'From what?'

'I got to be honest, Abigail. Every time I get really close to you, I feel like I-I—'

'Go on.'

Angelo looked around for kindling to start a fire. 'Look, if you don't mind, I'd rather be on my own right now. I have a lot of thinkin' to do.' Mr Jinx sat and extended his paw. 'Yeah, you can stay, boy. You're not the one that's confusin' me.'

By first light the encampment was alive with activity.

Captain Burke was talking to the lieutenant over by the chuck wagon as the men went about their duties. Tumbleweed and Abigail were resting against the rockface eating a hasty breakfast while they still had the chance.

'Ye want some chow?' the old man asked when Angelo finally showed his face.

'No thanks.'

About a mile from the camp, lined up on a hilltop, were a small group of Ulzana's warriors. On spotting them Angelo hustled over to the captain and lieutenant. 'Have you made your decision, Cap'n?'

'Oh yes,' said Burke. 'I know exactly what I'm going to do!'

'Good.' Angelo picked up the arrow that Burke had thrown to the ground the previous evening. 'Lift this in the air. They'll see it as a signal to come forward.'

Burke took hold of the arrow. Using both hands, he raised it above his head. 'Like this, mister?'

'Yes, that'll do it.'

Then, to everyone's amazement, Burke snapped the arrow in two.

Angelo snatched the pieces from Burke's hand. 'You sonofabitch, you're gonna get us all killed!' He held the pieces as if they were one and waved them in the air. The small group of Apaches turned their mounts and rode off. They never saw Angelo's signal.

'I must say, Captain,' Feathersham said stiffly, 'Your actions today will not go unnoticed. I'll be making a full report. If any of us get out of this alive, it will be no thanks to you.'

'Do as you will, Lieutenant. Just remember one thing. The colonel would have us both court-martialed if we'd handed over guns to the Apache.'

'Better to give 'em a few of our guns than to have us all butchered,' Angelo scowled. 'Leastways we'd get what we came for, the outlaws and the gold. Or had you forgotten about that?'

Burke took hold of his binoculars and followed the progress of the departing Indians. 'I'll think of some other way of getting the gold and the scum that took it, without giving up anything to those savages.'

'There's no talkin' to you, Burke. You're stubborn as a mule, and just about as smart.'

He stalked over to his horse and picked up his saddle.

'Leave it,' Abigail said as she handed him the reins to her horse. 'You can take mine, she's ready to go.'

'You best keep your head down and stay out of sight,' he advised. 'I'm goin' to try and talk to Ulzana, and see if I can salvage somethin' from this mess. If I'm not back within the hour, you'll know I've failed.' He climbed into the saddle. 'Tumbleweed, you look after Mr Jinx for me. He's a good dog when treated right.'

'Don't ye worry none 'bout the dug. Ye'll be back before ye knows it.'

Angelo swung the horse around and heeled the mare into a lope. He headed up the hill to where the Apaches were last seen. Even before he reached the summit, an arrow whipped past his head, and as he drew rein and hipped around, he spotted an Apache already stringing a second arrow to his bow.

He dismounted quickly and threw himself behind a rock, dragging his Colt from leather as he went. An arrow dug into the dirt next to his left thigh. He rolled over and saw that it was Ulzana himself who'd fired the shot.

Camila appeared beside the Apache leader. 'It would be wise to put away your gun.' She beckoned him to follow as she moved toward the large group of warriors. He holstered the pistol and cautiously tagged along behind her.

Ulzana kept a watchful eye as Angelo closed in on the warriors. The five captives were lined up close together, kneeling on the ground with their hands bound behind their backs with rope.

'Angelo, you have to help us, you're the only one

that can get us out of this mess!' Quincy pleaded.

Ignoring him, Camila said, 'Ulzana says you are either very brave or a fool to have come back after insulting him.'

Angelo directed his speech at Ulzana. 'It wasn't me that broke the arrow; it was that damn ass of a cap'n.'

'It does not matter. Ulzana has taken the actions of the soldier blue chief as an insult. Now he is after blood.'

Two warriors closed in on the five captives and dragged Jimmy to his feet. 'What are you goin' to do to him, you red sonsofbitches?' Tom bellowed.

One of the warriors struck Tom on the back of the neck with the shaft of his lance. Tom cried out and keeled over into the dust.

There was nothing any of them could do save watch helplessly as the two Apaches tied Jimmy spread-eagled to four stakes in the ground.

'You don't have to do this,' Angelo told Camila.

'An example must be made,' she replied. 'Now, go. And tell the bluecoat captain that his stupidity has just cost the life of this young one – and that his death will not be the last.'

Angelo climbed into the saddle as the small group of Apaches encircled young Jimmy and pulled out their knives. He took in the grisly scene, then swung around the corner of the rocks and made his way down the narrow trail, trying hard to block out the screams that followed him every yard of the way.

CHAPTER TWELVE

Abigail and Tumbleweed rushed to greet him as he stepped down from the saddle. 'Are you all right?' asked Abigail.

'Not as you'd notice,' he replied, handing the reins to the old man. 'Where's Burke? He's got a lot to answer for!'

Tumbleweed pointed to the lean-to he'd set up a little ways from the main camp. 'Burke can wait. You look like you need to be alone awhile. Thure's some coffee brewin', too.'

Knowing the old man was right, Angelo wandered over to the fire, took the weight off and then rolled himself a cigarette. Sensing his somber mood, Mr Jinx lay quietly beside him with his head resting on his lap. But try as he might, there was nothing Angelo could do to wipe out the sound of Jimmy's screams. He flicked the half smoked cigarette on to the fire.

Lost in thought, he failed to see Abigail watching him until he finally heard the jingle of her spurs as she turned to walk away. Then he broke his long, moody silence. 'No, wait! Abigail . . . stay a while. I reckon I could do with a little company right now.'

'Are you sure? Tumbleweed said not to—'

'I'm sure,' he cut in, and then he added in a low, choked voice, 'Tumbleweed didn't see what I saw out there.'

Mr Jinx lifted his head and watched as Abigail sat beside Angelo.

'Do you want to talk about it?'

'I reckon not.'

'Are you sure? It might help.'

'I watched a young man die out there and there wasn't a single damn' thing I could do to help him. Right now I don't feel too proud of myself.'

'You're a good man, Angelo,' she said. 'You'd have helped him if you could.'

'I know. But somehow that doesn't help.'

'It will . . . in time. Right now you're too upset to think straight.'

'Let's just talk about something else,' he growled.

She nodded. 'All right. Such as. . . ?'

He took his eyes off the flames and allowed them to settle on her. He thought, *Damn it, girl. If you only knew how I felt about you.*

Without warning she asked, 'Do you ever wonder what it would be like to soar up amongst the stars?'

The question did what she'd been hoping it would do – it distracted him from his miseries. 'There's lots of things I wonder about,' he replied, and then added hesitantly, 'For a start, I often wonder about you.'

'Me?' she asked. 'What do you wonder?'

'I wonder what you'd do if I kissed you again,' he said softly.

All at once she grew very, very serious, and when at last she broke the sudden silence, her voice came out softer even than his. 'Why don't we find out?'

Well, there it was. An open invitation. For a brief moment he was lost for words. He thought, *Well, what are you waiting for? Kiss her, you idiot. You might never get another chance like this.* But then her expression changed subtly, and he knew that she'd seen something in his eyes that he didn't even realize was there himself.

'No,' she said gently. 'Let's wait. This is neither the time nor the place, and when it *does* happen between us, I want both to be right. Besides. . . .'

'What?'

'Your mind's still out there, isn't it? With that poor man they killed.'

He put his eyes back on the fire. 'Yeah.'

'That will pass,' she assured him, and something

about the way she said it made him believe it completely. 'This dreadful *situation* will pass. And then it will be *our* time.'

'That,' he said earnestly, 'is something I look forward to.'

At the crack of dawn Angelo rekindled the fire and was busy preparing coffee when Burke strode over, looking distinctly ill at ease.

'A word, Angelo?' he said tersely.

Angelo met his gaze. 'I've got a couple of good ones for you, Cap'n. Massacre. Slaughter. Defeat.'

Burke's jaw muscles worked furiously, but he held his temper. 'We need to talk,' he said. He turned and walked off a few paces so that he could stare out across the prairie. Angelo, curious, went after him.

'The Apaches are watching us from the hilltop on our right flank,' said Burke. 'They could attack at any moment.'

Angelo nodded.

'Then I think it's about time we set our differences aside, don't you?'

He turned to face Angelo and offered his hand.

Angelo hesitated just a moment, then took it. 'Agreed.' He put his eyes on the distant slope. 'I've done a lot of thinkin' this mornin', Cap'n, and for what it's worth, I think you made the right decision. Givin' Ulzana the guns *would* be a big mistake.'

'Which leaves only one option,' said Burke. 'Let him try and take them – and make him pay heavily for the privilege.'

'Either that, or we could take the fight to *them.*'

'Attack Ulzana, you mean?'

'Well, it's that or make a run for it.'

Burke winced. 'Either way would be suicide.'

'That's why I think we'll go with one final choice instead.'

'Well, don't keep me in suspense, man. What is it?'

'You'll know soon enough,' Angelo replied mysteriously. 'Are there any boxes in the supply wagon that's big enough to fit the size of a rifle?'

'Yes, I should think so, why?'

'I'll need two of 'em.'

'What do you plan to do?'

Ignoring the question, Angelo continued, 'Move the supply wagon about a hundred yards out with the two boxes inside, along with a box of shells. Make sure you take the cover off the bows, so Ulzana can see what he's getting.'

'Are you proposing to trade with them?'

'I'm gonna *trick* 'em,' Angelo corrected. 'Rope ten of the horses together and have 'em tethered to the wagon. I'll do the rest. Oh, and before I forget, have a loaded rifle inside a marked box so I know which one to open.'

'You do know there'll be hell to pay if this goes wrong.'

'Cap'n, there'll be hell to pay if we don't at least try it.'

Burke thought for a moment, then turned and gestured Feathersham over and passed along Angelo's instructions. Feathersham gave Angelo a long look, then nodded and said, 'I'll see it to immediately.'

'What are *you* going to do?' asked Burke.

Angelo said, 'I'm gonna get me a cup of coffee, then make contact with Ulzana. And after that, I'll be hoping to hell that he takes the bait.'

CHAPTER THIRTEEN

Tumbleweed watched as his friend moved off toward the Apaches on the hilltop. 'He'll be back befer ye knows it,' he said, patting Mr Jinx's head.

Ulzana's men let Angelo get within fifty yards of the crest of the hill, just close enough to let him see the promise of death in the way they held themselves. There were a dozen of them, but no sign of Ulzana. Briefly he considered the wisdom of the course upon which he'd set himself. If it all went wrong, he could very well end up paying for it with his life.

He eased the gelding to a halt and yelled, 'Ulzana, I cannot see you, but I know you can see me. Look over toward the soldier blues, there is a wagon. Inside that wagon are guns and ammunition! There are also horses for you! Bring the yellow metal and the captives and we will trade! Now I will go and wait.'

He was slowly turning the horse back down the trail when a gunshot tore through the early-morning air. The gelding reared up, almost throwing Angelo into the dirt. 'Easy fella,' he said as he swung back to see Ulzana's silhouette rising from the jagged skyline, holding a rifle.

'I hear your words, Liga Ba'cho,' called Ulzana. 'Go. Soon we will follow.'

Rattled by the shot and knowing how easily it could have punched him out of this life and into the next Angelo started the gelding moving again, at the same slow pace as before. Up ahead, he noted, everything was in position.

Burke along with Feathersham, Sergeant Hogan and six troopers, were waiting by the wagon as Angelo reined in his horse and slid from the saddle. 'Lieutenant, when the Injuns turn up with the prisoners and gold, you take charge and get 'em behind the barricade as quick as you can.'

'Yo! Anything else?'

'Yeah, make sure your men don't do any shootin'. I don't want to be caught in crossfire.'

The wagon driver looked over his shoulder. 'What do you want me to do?'

'When I give the word, head for the barricade as if the Grim Reaper was on your tail.'

The driver nodded. 'Don't worry. Once I crack

the whip, you'd better hang on for dear life.'

Angelo eyed Burke, sitting on the tailgate, and joined him. 'I thought you'd be behind the barricade by now, ready to take charge of the gold and prisoners.'

'What, and miss out on you getting one over on that no-good renegade? No, I'll stick around here if it's all the same.'

'Be my guest.' Angelo sat patiently watching for the Apaches as he took a swig of water from his canteen. He noticed Burke was in rather a strange mood. Maybe their new alliance had something to do with it. Whatever it was, he was only too pleased that Burke was going along with the plan.

Tumbleweed moseyed over to the wagon and screwed his eyes at Angelo. 'Whut in tarnation's goin' on? That sumbitch corporal down thur's grinnin' like a jackass eatin' cactus and nobody's tellin' me nuthin'. It's like I wasn't even here.'

'What the hell are you doin'? Get back with the others.'

Tumbleweed lowered his head and began to saunter back toward the rest of the men, muttering darkly as he went. 'I might be old, but not too old to know whun I'm not wanted.'

'And keep Mr Jinx in check,' Angelo called after him. 'I don't want to have to worry about him neither.'

'Here they come!' someone shouted.

Ulzana and ten of his warriors came down the trail at a trot. In tow were the eight packhorses carrying gold, and the prisoners on foot with their hands bound behind their backs. Camila rode alongside the young Apache leader, who carried a lance with a white rag tied at the head.

'Remember, Lieutenant, get the gold and the prisoners over to the barricade as soon as I give the word,' Angelo said as he stood and followed Burke beside the two boxes.

The Apaches stopped a few yards from the wagon and dismounted. 'I see Liga Ba'cho has brought horses. Has he also brought the rifles?' Ulzana asked.

Angelo was at a complete loss as to why the Apache kept calling him by such a strange name. He looked to Camila for an answer. 'Liga Ba'cho?'

'You are named for your dog, white-eyes. Liga Ba'cho means White Wolf.'

Angelo rubbed the growth around his chin and smiled. He liked the idea of the Apaches giving him an Indian name. But after this day it wouldn't be a name they'd remember with any fondness. 'Yes, Ulzana, I have your guns.'

The young leader signaled one of his warriors to go take a look.

Angelo hadn't anticipated anyone else checking

the boxes. 'Whoa there!'

The Apaches froze, watching him suspiciously.

'The glory of holding the first rifle should go to you, Ulzana.'

Before the warrior could get close enough to inspect the rifles, Ulzana shouted something in his native tongue and the warrior stopped and rejoined his group. The young leader moved cautiously toward the wagon, shifting his gaze from left to right.

Angelo opened the box the lieutenant had scratch-marked with a piece of rock and pulled out the rifle. Raising it high above his head he yelled, 'Look, Ulzana. Fine rifles for you to take back to your people.'

Ulzana smiled. He jumped on to the back of the wagon and took hold of the rifle.

'OK, Lieutenant,' Angelo said evenly. 'You know what to do.'

The lieutenant and his men quickly moved off with the prisoners and packhorses.

Ulzana crouched and rested the rifle on the side of the wagon, then began rummaging through the box, obviously looking for more.

Angelo quickly came up behind the Apache and grabbed him by the hair. He yanked his head back, then to the side and followed through with a head-lock. Ulzana tried elbowing his attacker, but couldn't make contact as the grip around his neck tightened.

Angelo then skinned his six-shooter and thrust the barrel at the back of Ulzana's head. 'Hogan, get someone to take the horses back behind the barricade. And hurry!'

The warriors looked helplessly on, not daring to retaliate for fear of hitting their leader by mistake. Camila, however, rushed forward. 'What are doing? You're no different from the rest of the bluecoat pigs!'

Even though Angelo felt badly for the young woman, he could show no remorse for his actions. 'I'm sorry, *señorita*, but we can't allow your man to run loose with army issue carbines. Now, you're welcome to come with us, or you can stay right here. Either way, it's all the same to me.'

Ulzana growled, 'You think you can just take me, white-eyes?'

'I just did. But don't worry, I don't mean you any harm. As soon as we're well on our way to the fort, I'll let you go. These are my words of truth.'

Ulzana gave a little laugh. 'My braves will kill you all long before then, white-eyes, and these are *my* words of truth!'

Their exchange was cut short when Burke intervened. 'OK, mister, step aside! I'll take it from here. I'm going to show this renegade the error of his ways!'

As Burke undid the flap on his holster and pulled out his pistol, Angelo's blood went cold. 'Damn it, Burke!'

'Let him go!' said Burke. 'One wrong move and I'll *shoot* the heathen sonofabitch!'

'Captain, I suggest that whatever crazy idea you've got floating around inside that head of yours, you'd be wise to forget it.'

Ignoring him, Burke grabbed hold of Ulzana's throat and looking him in the eye said, 'You should have known better than to pit your wits against us, you red devil! You're mine now, and I'm going to make sure you hang high for your crimes!'

Angelo swore. 'I might have known you wouldn't miss the opportunity of taking a renegade like Ulzana back to the fort as your prisoner! Hunting glory, Burke?'

'Think whatever you like. One thing's certain. This savage's raiding days are over.'

Ulzana's warriors began moving closer to the wagon. Angelo knew it would only take one stupid mistake for the small band of renegades to get the upper hand.

Making a snap decision Angelo moved quickly, shoving Burke away from his prisoner and slamming him hard in the gut. Burke groaned and fell to his knees.

In the same moment an arrow skimmed the side

of the captain's head. A shallow furrow appeared as he fell sideways off the wagon and into the dirt.

The sudden attack on Burke distracted Angelo and Ulzana took full advantage of it. The Apache threw a punch that caught Angelo clean on the jaw and sent him reeling over the boxes and sprawling on to the wagon bed.

Ulzana was on him like the devil on sin. He dragged Angelo back up, kneed him once, twice, a third time, hard in the stomach. The air left Angelo in a rush and at least one rib popped. Suddenly he was powerless to defend himself and with sudden, unholy relish, Ulzana knew it. The Apache grabbed him by the ears, held him steady, rammed his knee up into Angelo's face. There was a jet of blood that stained the Indian's leggings, and then Angelo's eyes rolled up into his head.

The driver panicked when he saw what was happening, and with a swift snap of the reins brought the team into a frenzied dash.

The unexpected jolt unbalanced Ulzana and he fell to the side of Angelo, who was half-dazed but still trying desperately to get to his feet. The two exchanged blows as they were thrown around by the unsteady motion of the wagon, which was now heading away from the barricade. In the heat of the struggle, Angelo desperately tried to take control, but found it difficult to get the better of this young

Apache who was proving to be an even match for him.

The wagon slammed over a fold in the trail and Ulzana fell sideways, coming up hard against the wagon's sideboard. Angelo, clinging to consciousness for all he was worth, rolled over, pushed to all fours and then, hugging his busted rib with one arm, threw himself at the other man. The wagon rattled and shook as he landed on Ulzana, empty boxes slipping and sliding this way and that, and he punched him in the head.

The Apache snarled, shook his head as if he were trying to rid himself of a pesky fly, and made a clumsy grab for him. Each sought a hold on the other, but with the see-saw motion of the wagon it was like trying to fight on the deck of a storm-tossed whaler.

The wagon veered to the right, leaving the beaten track, and hit a steep incline which threw both men into the air. Angelo bounced heavily off the tailgate and on to the bed, knocking the wind out of him and finally knocking himself unconscious. Ulzana landed awkwardly and tumbled over the side, narrowly escaping the churning rear wheels.

Leading the Apache's pony to where he'd fallen, Camila reined her mount and jumped down to help her man to his feet. He grabbed the mane of his pony and heaved himself up on to its back, then headed toward his warriors.

Realizing the Apaches weren't giving chase and were, for the time being at least, no longer a threat, the wagon driver slammed on the brake and pulled hard on the reins until the horses came to a gradual halt.

Sergeant Hogan quickly made his way to the wagon and peered over the side at the unconscious Angelo.

Still shaking from the almost uncontrollable wild flight, the driver wiped the beads of sweat from his face with his kerchief. 'Looks like he's all done in, Sergeant.'

Angelo began to stir. He raised his hand to block the sun from his eyes and cringed as the sharp pain of a broken rib ricocheted through his body. 'What . . . what happened to Ulzana?'

'He decided he didn't want to stick around.'

'He's gone?'

'Yeah, he's gone all right,' Hogan said as he helped Angelo to his feet.

Angelo looked toward the horizon to see if he could catch a glimpse of the renegades, but saw nothing. He tried to take in what had happened. Only a few moments ago they'd had the upper hand. But once again Captain Burke's ability to disrupt well-laid plans without even trying was more than he could grasp.

'Ulzana won't let this insult slide,' he croaked.

They watched the lieutenant riding toward them on the captain's horse. Burke was lying unconscious over the pommel. 'Is he dead?' Hogan asked.

'No, but he's lost a lot of blood. Give me a hand to get him down from here. We need to stop the bleeding as quickly as possible.'

Hogan reached for the driver's canteen and poured a little water over his bandanna. After he'd cleaned the dirt from around the wound the captain began to stir.

'You're gonna be OK, Cap'n,' he said as he dabbed the moist bandanna over Burke's dry lips.

Feathersham tied the reins of Burke's mount to the rear of the wagon and climbed up and sat beside the driver. 'Try and keep him still, Sergeant. OK, let's move out.'

The driver released the brake lever, flicked the reins and the wagon moved off at a steady pace, heading for the barricade.

CHAPTER FOURTEEN

After carefully inspecting his wound Captain Burke glared at Angelo. 'I'll not forget what you did back there, mister,' he snarled. 'You almost got me killed!'

'Your damn' fool attempt to play the hero nearly got us *all* killed!' Angelo returned hotly. 'Christ Almighty, Burke, did you *really* think Ulzana's men would have given us safe passage out of here, knowing what you had planned for him when we reached the end of the trail? First chance they got – full dark tonight, like as not – they'd have hit us just as hard as they could. And why? Because they had no reason *not* to! They'd have wiped us out, all save one or two, whom they'd allow to survive only so they could take the story of what had happened back to the fort. The rest would be just about as dead as a man – or a woman, comes to that – can get!

Wincing with pain he propped himself against the side of the wagon. Knowing it was useless to reason with such a pompous ass, he decided the best thing for him to do would be to keep quiet and concentrate on regaining his strength for the conflict that lay ahead.

As Angelo limped off to join Abigail and Tumbleweed, Burke grabbed the front of Hogan's shirt and drew him close. 'I want that saddle tramp in irons, and put with the rest of the prisoners. No one's to talk to him, and that goes for Miss Abigail too. You got that, Sergeant?'

'He's got no such thing, Captain,' said Feathersham. 'That man is absolutely right on the money, sir. You jeopardized this entire company by what you did out there, and since you're clearly in no fit state to maintain command, I am taking over until further notice.'

Burke's eyes went wide. 'What? What was that?'

'You heard me, Captain.'

'Damn you, Feathersham, I'm wounded, not dead! I can still carry out my duties as good as any man around here.'

'Really, sir? It seems to me that that blow has severely impaired your judgement.'

'Why, you—'

'For once just do the decent thing and shut up, Johnny!' said Abigail, storming over.

'Who are you to take that tone with me?' Burke demanded.

'I may not have come from West Point, but I know the evidence of my own eyes. I know we are in the devil of a situation here and I know also that your actions have made it considerably worse! Turning Angelo into a scapegoat won't make it any better, and I will see that my father hears the truth of this as soon as we get back to the fort!'

Burke bridled. 'I resent the implication of your words—'

'That is because the truth has a habit of *hurting*!' she replied forcefully.

Lieutenant Feathersham gave her a sympathetic smile, then turned to Burke and said, 'She's right, sir. You made a mistake. A wise man would own up to it and make sure it doesn't happen again.'

Burke looked angrily at him. 'Let's get one thing clear, mister. Just because you pulled me out of harm's way back there doesn't give you the right to dictate to me what I should or shouldn't do.'

'Perhaps not. But may I respectfully suggest that you look to your responsibilities toward the men under your command, sir. They in turn are looking to you for leadership. With the right leadership they may survive this nightmare. Without it they may decide to follow someone who inspires greater confidence.'

Burke's eyes bugged. 'Good grief, man, you're talking mutiny!'

'I am merely pointing out what could happen, sir, if you don't get down off your high horse and start thinking about others instead of yourself.'

Burke's mouth opened and closed a few times. 'I'll see you court-martialed for that remark!'

'Please do, sir. I shall be more than happy for this entire story to come out in the open.'

'Enough!' Burke yelled.

'Yes,' said Feathersham. 'More than enough. Now, get some rest. As of this minute I am assuming command. If you don't like that, sir, I suggest we put it to the vote. Then you'll see just how popular your leadership has made you!' He turned and fixed Hogan with a glare. 'Sergeant, detail a couple of men to guard the captain. I want him watched at all times, and I'll hold you personally responsible if he gets in my way.'

As night approached the camp was in a state of vigilance. Lieutenant Feathersham secured the perimeter while everyone else cautiously went about their duties. Several of the troopers led the horses down by the river to drink, and those who were stood down played cards or grabbed some well-earned sleep.

A young trooper who was guarding the prisoners sat with his back against a water barrel, playing his mouth organ.

After tending Angelo's wounds and strapping up his ribs, Abigail snuggled up to him and listened to the tune the young soldier was playing. 'What a pretty tune,' she remarked.

The trooper nodded. 'Yeah, my father taught it me. The tune and this here mouth organ is the only memory I have of him since he passed on.'

Abigail looked at the young soldier with empathy. 'I'm sorry to hear that.'

'Oh, it's OK; it was way back in 'sixty three. He was killed at Chattanooga, crossing the Tennessee River under the command of General Thomas. Ma said he was a hero. But I guess there were a lot of heroes that day.'

'Yeah, I guess so.' Angelo dug into his shirt pocket for the makings and rolled a cigarette. 'You got a light?'

The trooper pulled a match from his pocket and struck it against the stock of his carbine. Angelo leaned forward and lit his cigarette. 'Thanks. That tune, what's it called?'

' "Going Home". I can play it again if'n you like?'

Angelo gave a curt nod and the young trooper

put the instrument to his mouth and began playing. Some of the troopers gathered around to listen. Taking into account all that had happened over the past few days, it was hard to believe how serene the atmosphere was around the camp.

Abigail stood and began to sing along to the music.

There's a place in my mind, that I'm hoping to see.
It's far, far away, made for you and for me.
I know in my heart, if we get through this fray.
The struggle will be over, at the break of the day.

'Thanks, miss,' the trooper said, clearing his throat with emotion. 'My ma used to sing it to me, just like that, when I was a kid.'

Abigail smiled and gently patted him on the shoulder. 'You're welcome.'

'Oh, so damn touchin'. It makes me wanna puke,' Tom Randall said, spitting to the side.

Quincy laughed. 'Yeah, and before you know it, the big fella here'll be playin' house.'

Angelo locked his gaze on him. 'Why don't you save your jokes for Ulzana, Quincy? He might find 'em a lot funnier than I do.'

Tom looked over Quincy's shoulder. 'Ulzana! Ha, we've seen the last of him. I mean . . . I heard someone say he'd run off with his tail between his legs.'

'You can believe what you want,' Angelo said. 'But I figure Ulzana is plannin' his next move even as we speak.'

'All the more reason why you should think about our original plan!' Quincy offered.

'Meanin'?'

'Hobble your tongue, Quince,' Tom snarled. 'We don't need him.'

Not shifting his gaze, Angelo said, 'Oh, I get it, you're still plannin' on makin' off with the gold, huh?'

Quincy winked. 'Why not, big fella? The renegades are pissed at the soldier boys, not us.'

'Yeah, let's put our differences behind us, and get the hell out of here,' Frank said, holding out his bound wrists. 'C'mon Angelo, what do you say?'

'You're not going to listen to them, are you?' asked Abigail.

'You of all people should know that I wouldn't go back on my word. I made a promise to your father and I intend keepin' it.'

'Then to hell with you, mister,' Quincy barked. 'You can rot, as far as I'm concerned.'

Just then Tumbleweed came over with Mr Jinx by his side. The dog lay at Angelo's feet while the old man crouched, then pulled out his pipe and tobacco. 'It's such a darn peaceful night, tonight.'

Angelo nodded. 'Yeah, it's a pity, there's a storm

a-brewin'.'

'Storm? I don't see nuthin',' Tumbleweed said, looking upward. 'It's so darn clear.'

'I wasn't talkin' about the weather, old man. Those renegades are out there. I just know it. I can feel 'em watchin' us.'

The old man edged closer to Angelo. 'I wish ye wouldn't talk like that, young 'un, yer givin' me the willies.'

'Yeah, well with that in mind, it'll be best if'n you keep your wits about you and your gun close by your side.'

In the early hours no one saw the dozen Apache warriors crouching in the shadows north of the camp. Ulzana's eyes narrowed as he picked out a target in the moonlight and then released the bow-string, which sent an arrow hurtling toward his unsuspecting victim.

Ryan, the bucktoothed kid, gasped in horror as he stared at the shaft protruding from his gut. The metal arrowhead dripped with blood as he keeled over.

The remainder of the prisoners panicked, and huddled up behind the wheel for cover.

'Jeez, Quincy, we're sittin' ducks here!' Frank shrieked as an arrow skimmed overhead.

Tom pulled frantically at the chains. 'For

crissakes, somebody, get us out of here!'

The lieutenant, with his pistol drawn ran toward them. He called to a trooper who'd taken cover behind a rock, 'Help me get them loose!' The lieutenant managed to get one of Frank's wrists free when Sergeant Hogan came barging over.

'What the hell are you doin', sir? The cap'n gave strict orders they were to remain in chains, no matter what.'

'It may have slipped your memory, Sergeant, but I'm in command now, not the captain. Now get out of my way and let me get on with it.'

'I can't let you do that, sir.'

The moment the trooper freed Tom from his shackles an arrow hit him in the chest. He cried out as he slumped forward and died. Tom reached down for the key then quickly began to free Quincy.

The lieutenant glared at Hogan. 'Sergeant, I don't have time to argue about this!'

The lieutenant went to open the remaining metal cuff on Frank's wrist, when Hogan grabbed hold of him by the shoulder and punched him square on the jaw, knocking him off his feet.

Abigail gasped as she watched the lieutenant's head bounce off a rock where he landed. 'Have you taken leave of your senses, man? You've just struck an officer,' she yelled, as she rushed to the lieutenant's aid.

Hogan pushed past her, but was taken aback when Angelo came at him swinging wildly with his fists, one of which caught him hard in the gut. He let out a deep groan, then, catching his breath, retaliated by grabbing Angelo by the throat and looking cruelly into his eyes. 'That's gonna cost you, mister!' he grated.

Angelo felt a sharp bolt of agony when Hogan prodded at his busted rib.

He dropped hard on to one knee, and there was nothing he could do to stop the irate sergeant from rushing off toward the horses.

Tumbleweed and Abigail dragged the unconscious lieutenant out of harm's way over by a clump of rocks, while the prisoners collected weapons from the dead and took up defensive positions. Quincy crouched in front of Angelo, blazing away with a six-shooter at anything that moved among the shadows.

'You don't look too good there, big feller. By the time this little skirmish is over you might be beggin' us to include you in our little plan.'

'Go to hell!' Angelo yelled above the gunfire.

'Have it your way.' Quincy laughed. 'I won't be askin' again.'

'Glad to hear it.'

'Do ye wants me to put a bead on that no-good sumbitch sergeant? I can plug him from here. Just say the word.'

Angelo thought for a moment, then decided that a quick death from a Sharps carbine would be an injustice. No, Angelo wanted to see this bully squirm a little before he walked through the gates of hell. 'Leave him to me, old man. You just concentrate on looking after Miss Abigail and the lieutenant.'

'Ye got it, young 'un.'

Hogan saddled up one of the mounts and shiftily looked around before securing the bulky saddlebags.

Angelo watched with curiosity. Hogan might have been many things, but Angelo hadn't pegged him for a coward, so why was he attempting to ride out under the cover of darkness while the whole camp was in disarray?

The noise of gunfire and the war cries from the Apaches spooked the horses. They pulled back, trying to free themselves from the rope to which they were tethered. Hogan's horse reared up, almost throwing him from the saddle when a trooper stepped in and grabbed the bridle with both hands.

'Easy there, boy. It's OK, Sarge, I've got him.'

Hogan lashed out with the reins. 'Get out of my way, you damn fool,' he yelled, then spurred the gelding forward.

He didn't get far.

Ulzana released an arrow from the darkness that whacked the sergeant in one beefy shoulder. As he cried out his horse stumbled and he fell from the saddle. 'Sonofabitch!' he yelled.

Before making their way back into the night shadows, Ulzana signaled to one of his men to finish off the helpless sergeant.

The renegade was only too happy to be given the chance to snuff out the life of this vulnerable blue-coat. He ran forward with his knife unsheathed until Hogan could almost smell his sour breath. He struggled to open the flap of his holster, but his attempts were in vain as the steel of the long blade cut deep into his flesh, slicing him from ear to ear.

The renegade threw up his arms and gave a triumphant yell. Two rounds in the chest from Angelo's pistol made sure his celebration was short-lived.

CHAPTER FIFTEEN

Half a dozen soldiers lined up behind the barricade and waited grimly for the second assault. The guard, who'd been on duty at the front of the wagons, lay dead with several arrows in his back. No longer under guard, Captain Burke ran up and down the line, yelling orders.

'Can ye believe that sumbitch?' asked Tumbleweed disgustedly. 'He's about as crazy as a lizard on a hot stove.'

'Yeah, maybe that head wound hit him harder than we thought,' Angelo said as he reloaded his pistol. 'How's the lieutenant doin'?'

'He's got a lump on his head the size of a turnip. He's conscious, but I figure it'll be a while before he's thinkin' straight again.'

'Damn!'

With the lieutenant out of action, Angelo knew

Burke would try to retake command, and in his present state of mind could prove to be their downfall.

'Would you believe it?' Quincy growled, looking at the gold bars that had spilled from Hogan's saddle-bags. 'The darn fool was tryin' to run off with some of our gold.'

That explained everything to Angelo. The sergeant had seen a chance to make off with the gold and had taken it – or tried to. 'Well, it did him about as much good as it'll do you, happen you stick to your plan. No good'll come of it.'

Quincy glared at Angelo. 'Well, we all know where you stand, big fella. Just remember when the time comes, keep out of our way . . . or you'll—'

'Enough!' Burke yelled, drawing his saber from its scabbard and raising it high. 'All right, you men, get ready to move out and be quick about it.'

The soldiers glanced at each other uncertainly. One of them said to Angelo, 'What do we do? I mean, I thought the lieutenant was in charge!'

Before Angelo could reply, Burke snapped, 'Well, you thought wrong! Now get those mounts saddled or you'll answer to me! Got that?'

'Stay where you are!' snapped Angelo. 'And that goes double for you and your boys, Quincy! In the first place, no one's about to let you ride out of here with that gold, and in the second, you'll be lucky to get all of a yard before Ulzana cuts you down!'

The trooper who'd been playing the mouth organ gestured with a trembling hand to the ridge south side of the camp. An instant later an axe split the back of his skull. A look of disbelief shadowed the young soldier's face as he slumped at Burke's feet.

Burke gulped. 'Take up defensive positions, we're under attack!'

'Ye don't say.' Tumbleweed said, reaching for his carbine.

Once again Ulzana and his men came out of the shadows, using whatever means they had to pick off their enemy.

One of the renegades charged forward with his knife raised high, ready to strike at Burke, who was unaware of the danger. The Apache let out a loud war whoop, and then lunged at the captain, who spun around and fell sideways into the dust. The Apache crouched, bringing the knife down in a murderous thrust.

Burke grabbed his attacker's wrist but the Indian fought back with everything he had. Seconds passed, and then Burke felt the tip of the blade prick his throat. Warm blood spilled and he immediately started to panic. Then, from out of nowhere, Mr Jinx leapt at the Apache, locked on to his forearm and drove him backwards into the dust.

Burke scrambled to his feet, retrieved his pistol, took careful aim and shot the warrior three times in the chest.

As the Apache twitched, Mr Jinx gave a short bark and ran off.

A renegade carrying a short lance managed to get inside the camp perimeter unnoticed by climbing down from a ledge, but was then taken by surprise when he came face to face with one of the soldiers.

They looked each other up and down. Then the Apache glanced at the soldier's carbine, which wasn't cocked, and made his move. He raised his lance and hurled it with such a force that it almost knocked the trooper off his feet as it sliced through his chest.

Kneeling behind the cook's supply boxes, Angelo discharged his six-shooter until he heard the dull sound of the hammer striking a spent cartridge. He felt around his gunbelt to replenish his pistol, but to his dismay realized he was out of ammunition. His timing couldn't have been worse. Ulzana and two of his warriors were advancing on him.

The renegade leader stopped in his tracks and fired his carbine, missing his target by inches. Angelo quickly rolled over to escape the arrow which another had released from his bow. It whizzed overhead and stuck firmly into the chuck wagon's water barrel. The third renegade was about to throw his knife when Ulzana grabbed him by the arm and spoke in his native tongue. The warrior looked fiercely at Angelo, then took off into the night.

Angelo couldn't understand what had just taken place. Ulzana had spared his life, that much was for certain. But why?

Mayhem around the camp grew more intense as the death toll mounted. Ulzana lowered his weapon. 'Liga ba'cho, I did not know it was you in my path. Earlier, you had my life in your hands, and you could have killed me but chose not to. Now I have spared *your* life, so we are even.'

Angelo gave a slight nod, knowing when and if they met again, things wouldn't be so friendly. He watched Ulzana and his companion dash toward the rocks and out of sight.

Another one of the renegades struggled to release the pistol from a dead soldier's clutches. He froze when he heard the sound of a loud snarl. His head whipped around, and looking over his shoulder he saw Mr Jinx running toward him. Before the warrior could get to his feet, the dog pounced, tearing fiercely at his flesh. The Indian shrieked and then tried for his knife, but it never cleared leather. A bullet from Tumbleweed's carbine drilled through his skull.

Even though Ulzana was nowhere to be seen, more Apaches joined the skirmish. Abigail snatched up a discarded pistol, checked to make sure it was fully loaded. She took aim and fired at the hostiles. Slow and deliberate, she kept on pulling back the hammer and squeezing the trigger. 'I think I got one!' she yelled.

The old man scratched his beard. 'Wull if'n ye didn't, yer sure givin' 'em somethin' to think about.'

The attack ended as quickly as it had begun when Ulzana and his warriors dispersed among the rocks.

'Cease fire!' Burke yelled. He dusted himself down and adjusted his coat and saber belt. 'Lieutenant, get the men ready to move out.' When there was no answer he narrowed his eyes. 'Where the hell is Feathersham? He should be here!'

A shout came from one of the troops, 'Sir, don't you remember? The lieutenant was injured!'

Burke gave a blank look. 'Ah yes, er . . . get the wagons loaded, we're moving out.'

'Liga ba'cho!' Ulzana yelled from a safe distance high up amongst the rocks. 'Liga ba'cho, I know you can hear my words! Tell the white-eyes chief to give us what we want . . . horses, guns and bullets! We have tested your strength! You are no match for us! Give us what we want, Liga ba'cho, or when the sun is next high in the sky, we will show no mercy!'

For some moments an eerie silence fell upon the encampment as Ulzana's words unsettled the men.

'Did you hear that, Cap'n?' a trooper yelled. 'We're dead meat, that's for sure. What we gonna do?'

'I'll tell you what we're *not* gonna do,' Angelo told Burke softly. 'We're not pullin' out. If Ulzana wants our hides so bad, let him come an' get 'em.'

'Angelo's right, Johnny,' Abigail said.

Burke studied for a moment. 'I can go along with that . . . for now!'

Angelo glanced at the silhouette of the hills. 'If Ulzana is true to his word, we've got until midday. That should give us enough time to come up with somethin'.'

Just then a heavily built corporal walked up to Burke and saluted. 'Sir, things ain't too good. We've taken heavy losses.'

'How many?'

'Seven dead, including Sergeant Hogan.'

Burke frowned. 'Hogan?'

'Yeah, the sumbitch wus tryin' to sneak off wuth some of the gold,' Tumbleweed drawled.

Looking at the Randall brothers, Burke sighed. 'It would seem we can trust no one where the gold is concerned. Did I overhear you saying something about leaving?'

'First damn' chance I get,' Quincy replied grimly.

'Very well. Corporal – get the prisoners secured for the night!'

Tumbleweed, with Mr Jinx by his side, went over to Angelo. 'That feller is two cents short of a dime. Whur the hell does he think they're goin' to run to? Ain't nothin' out thur but them savages. And I knows fer a fact, the Randall brothers ain't gonna chance runnin' into *them* again.'

CHAPTER SIXTEEN

The sound of activity around the camp stirred Angelo from a shallow sleep. The pain from his injuries seemed worse than ever. He opened his eyes and watched the soldiers go about their business.

With a smile, Abigail knelt and handed him a mug of lukewarm coffee. 'How are you feeling?'

He reached for the mug with both hands and took a sip. 'I'm getting' there,' he replied. 'What's goin' on?'

'Johnny is preparing to move out. He's had everyone up since the crack of dawn, packing everything away. Gramps has made space in the supply wagon for you and Lieutenant Feathersham.'

'What?'

'You can't ride. Not in your condition.'

'The hell I can't!'

Angelo heard footsteps behind him and turned as Tumbleweed came up. 'I see yer awake, young 'un. I've fed Mr Jinx and I've made yer a bed in the wag—'

'I know what you've done, old man.' Angelo cut in, tossing his blanket to one side and getting unsteadily to his feet. 'And I ain't gonna be caught lyin' in no bed when we're attacked.'

Abigail breathed an impatient sigh. 'And how do you expect to heal, may I ask, if you are being jolted around on the back of a horse?'

'She's got a point, young 'un,' Tumbleweed said. 'You got a busted rib there. Somethin' happens to bust it up some more an'—'

'Don't *you* start. My mind's made up. Now, I'd be obliged to you both if you stop fussin' and saddle my horse . . . seein' how I can't do it for myself.'

'He's as stubborn as a mule, Gramps. There's just no getting through to him.'

'Reckon yer right, missy. It'll be best if'n I saddle his horse.'

Abigail wagged her finger. 'Don't blame me if you end up with a fever or worse.'

Angelo couldn't help but smile. He gently grabbed her hand. 'I'll be fine, and I promise if I feel giddy I'll ride in the wagon. How'll that be?'

'Promise?'

'I promise.'

Meanwhile, on the other side of the camp, Burke kicked at Quincy's feet. 'OK, get up. Going against my better judgement, I'm going to let you ride without restraints. But as a precaution you won't be carrying any weapons.'

'Well, that's mighty decent of you, Cap'n,' Quincy hissed. 'Why don't you cut our throats and be done with it?'

'Don't push your luck, mister or I'll have you back in chains before you know it!'

Tom nudged his brother. 'Touchy, ain't he?'

Quincy frowned. 'Yeah, well it ain't funny, Tom. That sonofabitch is gonna get us all killed if we're not careful.'

Captain Burke opened the water barrel beside the chuck wagon, took a ladleful of water and poured it over his head.

Close by, a group of troopers were discussing their predicament. 'We've lost over half the troop since we started out on this patrol, and with only ten men left, it might be best if we use the prisoners to help us. I say give 'em guns, and to hell with Burke.'

Burke took a towel from the chuck table and dabbed his face, then walked over to the group. 'You, trooper! Any more talk like that and I'll clap you in irons, too! In the first place, no one here gives a hoot about what you think. In the second, we've got enough to worry about with Ulzana breathing down our necks, without having to worry about the Randalls back-shooting us as well!' He then yelled over to the burly corporal who was tending to the horses. 'Corporal, organize a burial detail, and be quick about it; we'll be moving out as soon as you're through.' He looked Angelo's way. 'What's the news on the lieutenant?'

'Why don't you check for yourself? He's in the supply wagon.'

As C Troop prepared to move out, Abigail took a canteen of water and some beef jerky and laid it on the wagon bed next to the lieutenant. She gave him a little smile as he began to stir.

'Where am I?' he asked, trying to sit.

'You took a nasty knock to the head.'

Rubbing his eyes, the lieutenant looked confused. 'I don't remember a thing.'

'Give it time, Robert; it will all come back to you. We'll be moving shortly, so try and get some rest. I won't be very far away if you need me.'

Burke peered over the tailgate. 'How is he?'

Abigail brushed his arm to one side and stepped from the wagon. 'I'm surprised you even care.'

'Why do you say that?'

'Don't pretend to be concerned, Johnny. I know you too well. The lieutenant's condition has given you the opportunity to seek the glory you crave for . . . and at what price, I wonder.'

Burke moved away from the wagon, and called out, 'Angelo, a word if you please.'

Angelo pushed back his hat. 'What is it?'

'If we move out now we'll have a good few hours' start on Ulzana,' said Burke. He pulled a map out of his saddle-bags and hunkered down to unfold it. 'See, we can't go back the way we came, it would be too dangerous. We need to cross the river to get back on track. It's too wide here, so we need to find a spot where it narrows and we can cross it quickly.' He pointed to an area on the map. 'Heartbreak Pass is about two miles north of here. Seems like the perfect place; it's only about fifty feet wide.'

Angelo studied the map for a moment, then looked towards the hills. He knew Ulzana would be watching and wouldn't let them get away so easily. No matter where they crossed the river, they would be vulnerable.

Tumbleweed crouched beside the two men. 'Heartbreak Pass, are ye crazy?' he demanded.

Burke glared at the old man. 'Now what?'

'I've heard stories 'bout that place, and none of 'em good. The river's deep and thur's strong undercurrents. Only a fool would chance crossin' thur, specially wuth wagons.'

Burke's impassive gaze switched from the map to the old man. 'Good. Then there's less chance of the Apaches following. Besides, if we cross the river there, it'll save us almost a day's ride.'

'I just don't believe ye! Is thur anythin' 'tween those ears of yers besides fresh air?'

Burke folded the map and pushed it into his saddle-bags, then mounted his horse. 'No one's asking you to come with us, old man. You're welcome to stay here if you want.'

'Sumbitch!'

Sliding the freshly loaded pistol from its holster and waving it at the prisoners, Burke raised his voice, 'You will all be riding point, with you, Quincy, leading the spare horses. That way I can keep an eye on you.'

Quincy spat. 'Well, that's very thoughtful of you, Cap'n. I'm overwhelmed by your generosity.'

Everything was packed away, and there were still two hours before Ulzana's deadline. The men were tired and morale was low. The ragtag company, which was now only a remnant of what it had once been, sat astride their mounts waiting for the order to move out.

Angelo's face showed deep concern as he led the bay mare over to Abigail. 'I don't want you ridin' in the wagon, so I've had one of the men saddle your horse. Be ready to ride like the wind if need be.' Placing his hands on her shoulders, he looked deep into her eyes. 'As soon as we begin to move, Ulzana will realize there's no deal, and attack. Stay close to me.' Giving Tumbleweed a curt nod, he said, 'You too, old man . . . stay close.'

Mr Jinx jumped up at him excitedly.

'Yeah and that goes for you too, fella. Don't you go wandering off, I might need you.'

The dog gave off a thunderous woof.

CHAPTER SEVENTEEN

Burke stood in the stirrups and raised his hand. 'C Troop, get ready to move . . . move out!'

They started off in single file with Quincy, Tom and Frank in the lead, followed by Burke, then his troopers with the wagons at the rear. Angelo, Tumbleweed and Abigail rode side by side, flanking the troopers to the left.

When Heartbreak Pass came into view, the driver of the chuck wagon let out a yell. Angelo looked back to see him falling into the dust with an arrow in his chest. Ulzana and thirty of his warriors were close on their heels, riding at full gallop.

'Burke, you'd be wise to dismount the men and take cover.'

The captain ignored the advice and shouted, 'Follow me, men!'

'Darn fool,' Angelo snarled. Not letting Abigail

out of his sight, he heeled the gelding into a gallop.

The clattering of hoofs and the churning of wagon wheels were drowned out by the high-pitched war cries from the renegades as they gained ground.

Burke was the first to reach the point of crossing, but his horse was reluctant to move off from the riverbank. It reared up, lashing out with its forelegs. The captain dug his heels hard into its flanks. It neighed in protest, tossing its head from side to side. Burke tried desperately to gain control. Thrashing the beast's hindquarters with the reins, he finally managed to urge the horse into the water.

'Sir, the renegades have taken the chuck wagon!' someone yelled.

'Forget it! Keep moving!' Burke called back as he went a little further into the river. He'd gone only a few yards when an arrow pierced his side.

Terror leapt into his eyes as he stared at the blood trickling on to his holster and down his thigh.

Angelo grabbed the reins of the captain's horse, turned and headed toward a mass of mesquite and large rocks with Tumbleweed and Abigail following. When they reached cover, Burke tugged at the arrow. His eyes rolled, his limp body slipped from his horse.

Angelo jumped from the saddle. 'Abigail! You take the horses. Tumbleweed, give me a hand with

Burke.' They dragged the captain over to a large boulder and propped him up.

A horse galloped into the enclosure, almost crashing into the rock face with two troopers on its back, one with an arrow buried in his shoulder. The rider climbed out of the saddle and helped his comrade dismount. They both scrambled for cover beside Captain Burke. 'I don't want to die!' the wounded man cried out.

'Shut up . . . no one's gonna die, you hear me?' his friend barked.

Frank rode low in the saddle trailing the supply wagon. At Angelo's insistence, the canvas cover had been removed in case of burning arrow attacks. As Frank got closer, he called out to the lieutenant, 'Throw me a gun, for Chris'sakes!'

Feathersham quickly glanced around the floor, but all he could see was the boxes of gold, sacks of flour and an array of assorted tools. 'I've only got my pistol!' he called back. 'Head for the rocks, I'll cover you!'

Frank never got the chance. A bullet tore through his knee and sent him reeling from the saddle and into the dirt.

The lieutenant crouched behind the sideboards, loosing off pistol fire at the Apaches. One of them fell over the back of his pony, blood gushing from a fatal head wound. Feathersham held on to one of the wagon bows and waited until the unmanned pony was close enough to reach. Then he swung around and jumped, landing awkwardly on its back. Seizing the mane with both hands, he turned the distraught animal and headed back to help young Frank.

The pony's hoofs threw up a cloud of dust as it was brought to a sudden halt. Lieutenant Feathersham leant forward. 'Give me your hand!'

The outlaw rolled around screaming as the blood flowed from his shattered kneecap. 'I can't!' he called out, struggling to get to his feet.

Feathersham leaped from the pony. 'Come on, we need to get out of here!' Using all his strength, he lifted Frank up on his shoulder and carried him to the clump of rocks where the others had taken cover.

When Burke came to he looked down at the arrow shaft jutting from his side. 'It's bad, isn't it?'

'It's not good.'

'Can it be removed?' Abigail asked worriedly.

Angelo shook his head in frustration. 'If I try, I might as easily kill him as save him.' He ran over to his gelding and pulled the rifle from its scabbard, then dove into the prone position, rapidly firing at the renegades.

The wounded trooper glared at Burke. 'You got us into this mess, you sonofabitch. I hope you're satisfied!'

Burke's irate expression was clear. 'Watch your tongue, trooper. Or by God, I'll have you court-martialed.'

The trooper snorted. 'You really think I give a damn? Take a look around you, Cap'n. This is all what's left of your precious C Troop. None of us are gonna make it outta here alive.'

Ulzana and his warriors charged after the stragglers who were out in the open. The driver of the supply wagon turned the team and headed for the river.

'No!' a trooper called out. 'You'll never make it, the current's too strong!'

The driver didn't hear him above the rattle and rush of wagon wheels.

Shouting over his shoulder to his brother, Quincy edged alongside the wagon, 'C'mon, Tom, here's our chance. The gold's ours for the takin'.'

Tom reined his horse to a slow trot and looked around. It seemed as if he were torn between following his brother or heading for cover with the others. The renegades closed in, throwing an array of missiles his way. The spinning blade of a tomahawk buried itself between his shoulder blades. He tumbled from his horse, kicking, screaming and trying frantically to reach the wooden handle. A warrior gave a loud whoop as he jumped from his pony and drew a knife that claimed the scalp of the dying outlaw.

The wagon team, meanwhile, struggled to pull the heavy load through the hazardous water. When Quincy came level with the driver he reached for the handrail and heaved himself up on to the seat, leaving his horse free to head back to the riverbank.

The driver gave the outlaw a quick glance, then focused on the task of controlling the skittish horses across the river.

Quincy looked over his shoulder and caught sight of the boxes of gold lying on the floor. His eyes lit up when he saw the loose bars that Sergeant Hogan had tried to make off with. He climbed over the seat, and picked one up and kissed it.

'What the hell are you doin'?' the driver asked. 'Get up here and give me a hand with the horses!'

Quincy reached down, picked up a shovel and slammed it against the driver's head. The soldier slumped forward, falling from the seat and landing between the charging horses. The shock pushed them further into deep water.

Quincy started picking up the loose bars and placing them in a canvas sack when suddenly water started flowing over the sideboards. He sprang to his feet, dropped the gold and lunged for the driver's seat. He looked in horror as he watched the horses thrashing about trying to keep their heads above water.

Without warning the strong currents dragged the wagon under, taking everything with it. All that was left of Quincy and the gold was a few ripples on the surface.

Partway along the trail Ulzana stood beside Camila, watching a handful of his warriors rummage through the contents of the chuck wagon. Several others rounded up the horses and collected the weapons from the dead.

Feathersham reloaded his pistol. 'We must look a pretty sorry sight about now.'

Angelo was inclined to agree but instead said: 'We can still give 'em hell.'

'What are they waiting for?' asked the wounded trooper.

This time Angelo didn't reply. Ulzana knew they were beaten. Now he planned to take his time finishing them off. 'How many rounds you got left, old man?'

' 'Bout a half-dozen.'

'I got about the same for my Winchester.'

'I still have my rifle,' said Abigail. 'And there's a full box of cartridges in my saddle-bags.'

Angelo hustled cautiously over to Abigail's horse. Mr Jinx followed him. As Angelo grabbed the carbine and shells he felt the dog's eyes on him. When he could stand it no more he looked down into Mr Jinx's face. 'You're a good friend,' he muttered thickly. 'You've pulled me out of a good few scrapes, and I'm grateful. But when Ulzana gets here, you better high-tail it.'

The dog lowered his head and offered his paw. Angelo took hold of it, glanced away, cleared his throat. 'Now don't think I'm goin' all soft on you,' he said. 'It's just a little dust in my eye is all.'

Mr Jinx wagged his tail, as if to say he knew better.

Watching the exchange, Tumbleweed sniffed and wiped his eyes with his shirtsleeve. 'I guess you have some dust in your eyes too, Gramps,' Abigail said softly.

'Shucks, missy. This is all my doin'.'

'How so?'

'Wull, if it hadn't bin for me and my big mouth 'bout the gold, we wouldn't be in this fix.'

'It's no good blaming yourself. We all had choices,' Abigail replied.

Tumbleweed shook his head. 'It's all bin fer nuthin'.'

Angelo squatted beside the old man and began loading the Winchester with fresh cartridges. 'I wouldn't say it was for nothin'.'

'How do ye figure?'

'For one thing, I found myself a good friend in you. You might be a pain in the butt sometimes, but that counts for somethin'.' Angelo caught Abigail's eye and winked at her. 'And I've also found someone very special. So you see, old man, the way I see it . . . it hasn't been for nothin'.'

'Wull, all I can say is yer one crazy sumbitch.'

'Liga ba'cho, Liga ba'cho, do you hear me?' Ulzana hollered.

Angelo glanced at Mr Jinx, Tumbleweed and then Abigail. 'Well, I guess this is it. Wait here, this is my call.' He stood, then walked out into the open. 'I hear you.'

Ulzana held a lance as he sat tall astride his pony. His cold eyes studied Angelo from head to toe.

'What're we waitin' for?' Angelo asked impatiently. 'Let's finish it!'

Ulzana hurled his lance. It stuck firmly in the ground several feet in front of Angelo. Angelo forced himself to stand tall and steady. 'Is that the best you've got?' he demanded. 'We've enough guns and ammunition to hold out for days, Ulzana. Many more of your warriors will die. Is that what you want?'

Ulzana grinned. 'The Apache could wait for days, until you are weak from hunger and you have no bullets for your guns. But we have taken what we came for. You are defeated, and in that I take great pleasure.'

Angelo frowned. 'So that's it? You're saying it's *over*?'

'It is over.'

'I thought the Apache way was to kill your enemy?'

'You thought wrong. There is nothing to gain by staying here.'

Angelo could see Ulzana's warriors moving down the hill toward them. Camila rode a horse taken from one of the dead soldiers. She stopped alongside her man, then looked over at Angelo and smiled.

Angelo touched the brim of his hat. '*Señorita.*'

Then he heard a sound behind him and glanced over his shoulder, his gut tightening unpleasantly when he saw Burke standing a few feet away. 'You want somethin', Cap'n?' he asked, narrowing his eyes, his tone ice-cold.

Burke didn't respond. He dropped to his knees and pointed a finger at Ulzana. 'I'm dying,' he managed, 'and you were my undoing.'

Angelo grimaced. 'Get back with the others. You're not helpin' any.'

Burke's eyes widened as he undid the flap on his holster and pulled out his Army Colt. 'What's up, Angelo? You taking sides with the savage?'

'Damn it, man, it's over!'

Burke held the pistol in a two-handed grip, thrust out in front of him to the full length of his arms. Beads of sweat formed on his forehead as he leveled it at Ulzana. He pulled back the hammer and put his finger on the trigger.

Angelo rushed at him, trying to ignore the pain in his ribs. 'Are you crazy?' he bellowed, knocking Burke off balance. The gun went off, but the bullet fell short of its target, spraying dust just inches from Ulzana's feet.

A look of hate shadowed Ulzana's face. He quickly dismounted and signaled to his warriors not to intervene as he walked toward Burke, plucking the lance from the ground as he did so.

Again Burke squeezed the trigger and to his dismay, heard the distinct sound of a hammer striking an empty cartridge. Not taking his eyes off Ulzana, he cocked the gun and squeezed the trigger again.

Nothing but a faint click could be heard.

Burke let the pistol slip from his hand. He looked around with pleading eyes, but no one made a move to help.

Ulzana passed Angelo and stopped only when his shadow draped Burke like a shroud. He prodded the captain with the tip of his lance. 'I cannot kill you, white man,' he said softly, and Burke gave a sigh of relief, hearing that. But then Ulzana looked meaningfully at the arrow in the captain's side and said flatly, 'You are already dead. You just don' know it yet.'

Knowing what Ulzana said was true, Burke's eyes

widened, he managed a single croak of sound and then keeled over, dead.

Ulzana stood proud, clutching the lance as he looked at Angelo. 'Now, it is over, Liga ba'cho. I will return to my people and you are free to return to yours. I will not forget you, white-eyes. Maybe we'll meet again someday.'

Angelo nodded. 'Maybe.'

The Apache leader remounted his pony and led his band of men towards the hills, heading west.

Abigail rushed to Angelo's side, breaking step briefly as she passed Burke. 'Are you all right?' she asked.

His eyes met hers. 'I am now,' he said softly.

Tumbleweed and Mr Jinx walked over to them. The dog sniffed at the captain's face and gave a little bark. The old man spat. 'Ye gonna bury the sumbitch, or whut?'

Angelo eyed the old man. 'I guess.'

Tumbleweed pushed back his hat and scratched his head. 'Good, the quicker we get him underground the better.'

Abigail's brow creased into a frown at the old man's remark.

'Whut?' Tumbleweed asked with a puzzled look. 'Wull, we don't want to be givin' those darn buzzards gut rot, now do we?'

An hour later shock began to set in. Angelo knew only too well that the long journey home would prove too much for some of them. The wounded needed medical attention, and without it the chances of infection were high. They were low on supplies, low on ammunition, and the outlook was bleak, the mood one of defeat and melancholy.

And then Mr Jinx pricked up his ears.

Angelo looked around. 'What is it, boy?'

The dog gave him a brief glance, then ran off toward the hills.

'Whut's gotten into him?' Tumbleweed said.

'Beats the hell outta me,' Angelo replied. 'At times he's a mind of his own.'

He sighed and went down to the river's edge, splashed water on his sweat-run face. It was hard to believe that only a few days ago he had been sitting by a campfire with Mr Jinx at his side, and neither of them had a care in the world as they'd watched an old man arguing with his mule.

'Mind if I join ye, young 'un?' Tumbleweed asked, following him down.

Angelo looked at him. 'If I remember correctly, those were the first words you uttered the night we met.'

'Whut?'

'Nothin'. Just reminiscin' is all.'

'Wull, ye can hark back to anytime ye want, but

the fact still remains. Because of me, all yer hard-earned cash in the bank will be turned over to the colonel for his school and hospital. Yep, losin' the gold really stinks.'

'Stop your complainin' and follow me,' said Angelo. He made his way over to the abandoned chuck wagon, climbed over the side, took out his knife and prised open one of the floorboards to reveal the gold bars.

The old man's eyes lit up. 'Huh? I don't understand!'

'Late last night I took the liberty of moving the gold. After Hogan tried to run off with some of it, I figured if anyone else tried the same thing, they'd be in for a surprise.'

'So ye hid it in here, eh?'

'Well, with the help of Feathersham and Abigail. I couldn't have done it all on my own, not with a busted rib and all.'

'Wull, ye sneaky young pup. Who would've thought it? Is it all there?'

'Except for the few loose ones taken from Hogan, yeah.'

Abigail looked sheepish as she walked over and took hold of Angelo's hand. 'Happy now, Gramps?' she asked.

'Only one thing'd make me happier,' he replied. And sobering, he said quietly, 'Standin' up as best man at your weddin'.'

Angelo glanced at Abigail. 'I got a feelin' the colonel might have something to say about that.'

'I'm not so sure,' said Abigail. 'You kept your word, Angelo. He'll have to take that into consideration.'

'Well, let's eat this pie one bite at a time,' said Angelo. 'We've got to get back to the fort yet, and that's not gonna be easy.'

Suddenly they heard barking in the distance. Angelo shaded his eyes and looked over to the northern ridge; there, to his amazement, he saw Mr Jinx running ahead of two columns of soldiers, led by an officer on a dapple-grey mount. Lieutenant Feathersham joined the young couple to find out what was going on.

Angelo gave Abigail a tight squeeze. 'Will you take a look at that? I don't believe it!'

'It's my father!' Abigail yelled tearfully. 'I'd know his horse anywhere! He's found us, Angelo! We're going home! We're going home!'